MW00893987

15 SHORT ROMANCE NOVELS

By. Mary M. Rose

2019

ISBN: 9781695380073

TABLE OF CONTENTS

INTRODUCTION

There are so many reasons to love short stories; not least their ability to immerse us in new worlds in the time it takes to commute to work, or the common themes that weave through anthologies to create a thought-provoking whole. Here, we've collated our edit of the best short story collections. From spine-chilling tales and funny short stories to literary masterpieces, these are simply not to be missed.

Want to know the best way to stuff your vacation full of as many wonderful stories as possible? Spend your summer reading a few of the new short story collectionsi've picked out for you on this book. Each of these collections packs plenty of great stories.

I'm a huge proponent of short fiction, particularly for book-lovers who find that their daily lives get in the way of their reading time. A novel might take you weeks to finish, depending on how demanding your work schedule is, but a short story can be squeezed into the few minutes you have to read each day. You can experience a full narrative, from beginning to end, every day. Pretty snazzy, huh?

Short fiction also gives you the chance to get a taste for a new author you may have been wanting to a read for a long time.

THE BACK STEPS

By Kevin Hughes

She was eleven the first time she met him. She had seen him around the street once in a while, but just on his bike, or walking with Big Eddie. Big Eddie was eleven too, but he was almost six feet tall- and so everyone called him Big Eddie. Not her. She always called people by their name. She knew (even at eleven) that sometimes nicknames hurt. She just thought it was tough enough to be six feet tall in the sixth grade, let alone having that pointed out every time someone called your name. So she called him: Eddie.

The kid walking with Big Eddie, or riding alone on his bike, was cute, but very quiet. She knew they went to the same school, but that was about it. He wasn't in any of her classes, and they didn't have any mutual friends. She wasn't even sure why she even noticed him, or why he was on her street. Big Eddie lived two blocks over, and she thought the quiet kid lived on the street behind her; so there wasn't any real reason for the cute quiet kid to be on her street in the first place.

So she was surprised to see him climb over the fence behind her yard and walk slowly towards her. Surprised enough to stop the flow of tears that were running down her face and leaving wet water marks on the old wooden boards below her feet. She was sitting on the top step of her back steps, as the cute quiet kid walked up next to her. Standing next to the steps and with her sitting on the top step, he was just a little shorter than her. But their eyes were almost even with each others.

"You okay?"

She could only nod.

"Do you need a shoulder to cry on? Mine is waterproof."

He opened his arms in a gentle gesture of "come here, be safe, and cry" manner. So she did. She leaned up against him, feeling his heart beat through the thin shirt he was wearing. He didn't have much muscle on a too thin chest (which she snuggled up against) as his arms folded across her back like a warm quilt, or an afghan knitted by someone known to you, and that you loved. He leaned his chin on the top of her head, and surprised her by humming a tune that sounded a lot like a lullaby.

She cried.

*****

She was fifteen now. Big Eddie was still only six feet tall and still walked with the quiet cute boy who lived on the street behind her. The cute quiet boy was still short. Shorter than her by more than three inches. When he came to visit, or talk, or just hangout on her back steps, she had to sit on the second step down so that she wouldn't be way taller than him. He had a little bit more muscled chest now. It muffled his heartbeat just a little when she snuggled into his arms as he stood next to her on the back steps.

5

He had a light dusting of down on his top lip now. She knew it wouldn't be long before he grew a bit taller, gained some more muscle, and lost his high child's voice. In the last four years she had grown use to that soft tone he used when speaking to her. Many times she would come out on the back steps feeling blue, or angry at her mother (who seemed not to understand what it was like to be fifteen, pretty, and confused). He would come over to where she sat and say:

"Do you need a shoulder to cry on? Mine is waterproof."

Sometimes that was all she needed. She would laugh and they would talk. Other times it wasn't enough. He would open his arms with that same "come here, be safe, and cry" manner that she had come to count on over the years. She would lean into his too thin chest, feel the comfort of his heart thumping a regular "it will be alright" message to her. Then he would hum. She would just let him hold her while she cried and for a while after she stopped crying too.

Sometimes he sat next to her - she didn't need a hug, comfort, or to cry. She just needed someone her own age to talk with. Someone she could tell anything to without being judged, misunderstood, or ridiculed. He always listened. He believed her. She knew it. So she told him everything.

*****

It was the night after her Prom. She was scared to go sit on the back steps. Scared that he might be there, more frightened that he

6

might not be. For she needed to cry tonight. She needed to talk tonight. She needed to be safe...tonight. She didn't think she would lose her virginity in the parking lot at the Prom; but Willy and her had been dating all through High School. So it seemed okay as passion overtook them both. But now she was scared. "What if I am pregnant?" was on a loop in her head...loud and constant.

She opened the door and sat on the third step down, so that if the cute quiet kid showed up (Please! Please! Please God, let him show up!) they could be eye to eye with each other. Him standing -as he always did- next to the back steps. Her sitting on the third step down, that made them even in height.

For when the quiet cute kid went through puberty, his voiced deepened, he had to shave (at least his top lip) but he only grew a few inches. At eighteen, he stood only five foot three. Her five foot eleven frame dwarfed his - even in flats. Willie was six foot four and her boyfriend - well, at least until last night. But the quiet cute boy was the bigger man.

*****

It was quiet out. One of those long Spring Nights that held onto the last of the sun, letting darkness trickle in slowly. She sat on the steps, forlorn, lonely, and upset. Last night she had given herself to Willie in a fit of passion. Today Willie and her had broken up. Willie would be okay, he was leaving for College Summer Session (for Scholarship Football Players, like him). But she had a long two weeks to think about whether or not she was going to have a period. She was surprised how "making love" with Willie, had proved to her that she did not love Willie at all. It was a surprise to them both.

And so she sat, as darkness leaked in around her. And then…

*****

He was there. Slowly walking from her back fence towards the back steps. He stopped next to her - almost eye to eye- and in the softest, kindest, most caring tone she had heard from him in the last seven years, he said:

"Do you need a shoulder to cry on? Mine is waterproof."

It was all she needed to hear. His arms opened, as they always did, with that warm "come here, be safe, and cry" invitation. She crushed herself against his chest. Pressing her head so tight against him that her breathing began to synch with his quiet in and out breaths. Like waves lapping up against the shore, each breath of his seemed to wash away the worries, thoughts, and fears she had harbored for the last night and day.

When he hummed, the last of her worries left. She slept.

*****

It had been eight years since she had been home. She had left town the next morning after she slept (sitting up) in the arms of the quiet cute boy. She took her Aunt Sylvia up on her invitation to spend the summer in New York City. The City turned out to be

8

the perfect place for her to fit in. She soared in the Art Community there. Her work made her World Famous. Rich. A celebrity. Her short lived marriage (less than three months) got her face plastered over a dozen gossip rags, and sound bytes on most Major Networks. The Publicity took its toll on her health, her business, and her heart.

At twenty six, she was an Artistic Superstar, a Business Success, an Influential Woman, and respected. In her own mind though she was just an emotional basket case with a failed marriage, a lack of conviction in her work, and a woman suffering from spiritual melancholy. Lonely. Alone. Depressed. In the middle of having it all, she found she had nothing. So she went home to …well… she didn't know why. She just wanted to sit on the back steps again.

The Town hadn't changed much. Big Eddie was still six feet tall, and the Manager of the local Costco. Willie used his fame as a Football Player to parlay his career into owning a string of Car Dealerships. Her Mom still owned the small house with the old planked back steps on it. She had no idea what had happened to the cute quiet kid since that night she slept in his arms, while sitting up.

Her Mom had fussed over her all day. They had a long talk, went out for lunch, and even got in a thrift shop or two. It was nice. It went a long way towards convincing her that she was smart in coming home to recharge her batteries, forgive herself, or lighten up. She wasn't sure which. When her Mom went to bed at

Nine PM (as she always did) - she opened the screen door on the back porch, and sat on the back steps.

Unconsciously, without any real thought, she sat on the third step down. It made her smile. She even spoke out loud:

"Oh, sure, Brandy. Sit on the third step down so you won't be taller than the cute quiet kid when he shows up to ask if you need a shoulder to cry on. Like he is going to be here after eight years."

It made her chuckle in a sad sort of way. Which is why the Voice made her nearly jump out of her skin.

"Do you need a shoulder to cry on? Mine is waterproof."

What happened next was too private, too personal, too perfect to tell you.

So I shall end there... at the beginning.

THE BREAKUP CAFE

By Akshay singh

Year 1999, when there were no breakups, only heart breaks.

It was 2:30 AM and Arjun kept checking his phone. He was sitting on a chair with his legs propped on the table. The table was neatly arranged with a few books from his college days and a notepad that he always kept with him to write stories and poetry. He was swinging a pen in hand impatiently. He kept thinking about the time it started and how surreal it felt then. He remembered when they went for a drive and it started raining and how they sang their favorite song together, but now things had changed.

He said to himself, "She does not deserve me anymore. It's over." Suddenly the phone beeped, and Arjun pounced at it.

The message read, "Alright! Let's meet for one last time at 10AM." The meeting point was their regular coffee joint where they first went 2 years back and ever since they went there almost every day.

Arjun was working in an IT company, but he always wanted to be a writer.

On the other hand, Nishka had her priorities sorted. She wanted to start her own Playschool and was accumulating funds while working at her current job.

Arjun thought to himself, "So she seems to have made her mind this time". He was not sure if Nishka had sent that message or someone else. They had many fights in the last two years for all the reasons a couple could fight. Every time a fight happened, Nishka would make things right. Arjun would later realize that he could have controlled his anger and maybe not overreact every time.

"If she does not care anymore it's better we breakup tomorrow; I need a closure," Arjun said out aloud as if trying to tell the same to Nishka. He went to sleep thinking Nishka must have slept so why should he lose his sleep over her. He could not sleep the whole night though.

So, the sun rose, Arjun was feeling sleepy but managed to get ready and started to drive from his house to the cafe. He kept on murmuring something as if revising the things he would say to her.

Arjun parked his car outside the cafe and went inside, trying to make the facial expression that would be appropriate for the situation, but he was unsuccessful.

He went straight to the table they would usually choose to sit, it was right in the middle with just two chairs and a white table. After 15 minutes Nishka entered the cafe, that made Arjun angry.

Nishka would often get late by 15-20 minutes whenever they planned to go out on a date and Arjun never liked any of her excuses.

Arjun behaved like a true gentleman. He got up from his chair, greeted her with a hug and pulled the chair for her, however, avoided any eye contact with Nishka.

Theirs was not a fairy tale kind of a love story but Nishka would always say that their relationship was very different. Arjun had been in a few relationships before but he never felt what he felt with Nishka.

As always, Arjun ordered his hot coffee and Nishka ordered a cold coffee.

No one wanted to initiate the conversation. Arjun started to visualize how his life was going to be from tomorrow without her. He was sure that their relationship would end today, as Nishka had always been the protector of the relationship at such times. Arjun looked at her while she was sipping her coffee and he realized that he wanted to grow old with her no matter how much he hated her now. He had never been that afraid in life to love or to lose. All this while, Nishka either looked at her coffee or just faced downwards with tears almost not visible in her eyes. He was about to fall in love with her all over again. Arjun was shocked to notice that Nishka was not even attempting to set things right this time around. After a few minutes, Arjun broke his silence and said, "If it's over, I wish u a happy life ahead." Nishka remained quiet. Her silence made Arjun angry. He stormed out of the cafe and waited near his car for 2 minutes. Every time something like this happened, Nishka would run and stop Arjun, but not today. Neither she came out nor she called. Arjun got angry thinking that she does not even care if he left from there. He went back furious, stood in front of her and said, "I knew you will not even bother to come out to say goodbye, so I will say it, Goodbye".

Nishka broke down in tears and that may be exactly what he wanted because she might speak to him now. Arjun's heart knew that now she would make things right and all Nishka ever wanted from Arjun was that he does not give up on her, just once. Arjun recalled all the fights that usually did not last for more than few hours. But, this time Arjun was astounded as Nishka said "Goodbye" in return.

Arjun was angry, his blood boiling but extremely broken and lifeless from inside. He placed his car keys on the table and fell on his knees. They both did not say a single word. Arjun held Nishka's hand and said sorry. He was just a few moments away from losing the love of his life. Tears rolled down Arjun's eyes. He got up and kissed her on her forehead.

Arjun looked at her for one last time with the hope that she would look back but Nishka remained quiet, still looking down. Arjun then left.

This was it, it was over. A relation of 2 years came to an end.

Year 2018:

Akshita was dressed in her school uniform. She was a little nervous but extremely happy as she was all set to read out her written story for the first time in the School auditorium. She had waited for long for this day. The stage was set, the auditorium was full, but she kept looking at the main entrance. The organizer called her to the stage and she walked up to the stage eyes still fixed on the entrance gate. Suddenly a man dressed in a business suit entered and Akshita calmed down. He signaled her to start and Akshita started to read. After a few moments of reading, Akshita was lost in her story. Everyone seemed to be shocked by the way she had written, it did not seem a 16-year-old girl could have written this. And when she ended the story, everyone started clapping and gave her a standing ovation for her extraordinary talent.

Akshita thanked everyone and started walking down the stage. Everyone sat back on their seats and the organizer was about to call the next participant. Suddenly in that moment of silence, someone started clapping from the main entrance, Akshita looked at the main entrance with joy while Arjun did not even look back and shook his head in disbelief as he knew it was Akshita's Mother who had a habit of reaching 15 minutes late.

Akshita ran towards her Mother and hugged her tight.

"Mom you are late again", said Akshita, to which her mother Nishka replied, "You don't get a day off in a playschool, imagine managing 50 kids like you!" Nishka teased her.

Arjun too joined them and they all hugged like one happy family. Akshita kept on talking about how nervous she was and how relaxed she is feeling now.

Arjun was happy to see his daughter living his dreams of becoming a writer. Nishka looked at Arjun and could see tears in his eyes.

Nishka held Arjun's hand and said "Thank you for not giving up on me that day"

Arjun smiled and remembered the cafe that got them back together.

THE END

DEPARTMENT OF CHANCE ENCOUNTERS

By Kevin Hughes

It was busy at Cupid Central. Perhaps 1 million or so hummingbirds or 2 million bees would make the same gentle buzzing sound in the background; but they wouldn't be anywhere near as cute as the dozen or so Cupids flitting about their duties. If there is anything cuter in the air than a Cupid with a full quiver headed out to their assignments for the day, well, Nature hadn't found it yet.

Quivers, of course, were verboten in Cupid Central. Ever since that time at the Office Party when tiny little Tina and Burt Bigelow decided to shoot Cupids instead of Humans. Let's just say the Big Boss had a heck of a time sorting who was in love with who. For almost a century Humans went without loving connections, Romance, and deep feelings - they had two World Wars, a Cold War, and enough Regional Warfares to splinter the Earth during those hard times.

Tina and Begelow, well they still haven't gotten their Quivers Back. They were excellent "Potential Spotters" though, so they did get to flit around Earth looking for potential Romance that - given a chance- could allow a Cupid to take aim. And so it is we begin our story.

*****

Tina soared through the Arch (There are no doors in Cupid Central- you either come in thru an Arch, or an open window). Burt Bigelow was right on her heels. Burt was aptly named, as he was quite chubby (in an angelic Rubenesque way), but it didn't matter; for Cupids can fly as fast as love can strike no matter how much they weigh, or how little their wings are.

In the "Old Days" before that fatal Office Party, Tina and Burt often went out together to target life long loves. In Cupid Central, both were legendary for finding the exact right Love, for the perfect Human Bonding. Heck, Tina and Burt combined for seventeen of the longest, most delightful, continually deepening Loves in Human History. Seventeen out of the Top Twenty. Think about that for a second. For Tina and Burt to hit you with an Arrow, easily gave you thirty to forty years of Wedded Bliss. No other Cupid Team in History comes close.

NOTE: If you are Human and reading this please understand that Cupids make mistakes too. Sometimes only one arrow lands squarely in the "True Love" zone of the heart. Often an arrow will narrowly miss "True Love" and you end up with a Summer Love, A fling, or (in the saddest of all Loves): "I don't think of you that way, you are more like a Big Brother - or Sister."

Some arrows miss all the Love Zones, and hit Fondness, Friendship, or Buddy Zones instead. That is okay with most Cupids, for True Friends are only slightly less rare than True Loves.

*****

Tina settled in the air with a little puff of Angel breath (which smelled like Lilacs). A moment later, a soft flutter, and Burt too arrived with a puff of Angel Breath (but his smelled like fresh baked chocolate brownies). They hovered there waiting for the Head of the Department of Romance to end her conversation with two other Cupids. It seems they had read the Forecasts for the week, and thought there was a pretty good Chance of Romance building up over Central Manhattan due to the snow storms.

Snowstorms and Good Weather at the Beach, are two of the most likely places for Romance to bud. In snowstorms, everyone crowds into Coffee shops, so a gentle nudge of an elbow, a drop or two of spilled coffee, and a Cupid has a clear shot from the Apology, or the proximity, to form at least a Casual Acquaintance. An offer to buy another coffee, or a slight widening of the eyes and an experienced Cupid can choose an Arrow that will lead to a Romantic Tryst.

At the beach, well, lets just say that curved youthful skin covered with a nice oily shine of sunscreen allows most Cupids to empty their Quivers in just a morning! Most Cupids don't take True Love arrows to the Beach, just weekend fling shafts- or lighter Summer Loves. In Snowstorm Cafe's though, the much heavier Serious Relationship, even Marriage arrows are used. In a bit of Irony, many couples aren't open to the piercing penetration of a True Love Arrow until AFTER they have been married for a while. You have to be open to True Love, or the Arrows just bounce off and fall to the ground.

Anyways, back to our Story.

19

*****

"Ahem." louder: "Ahem." Finally Burt just ignored Tina's gentle polite interruptions of the Chief of the Department of Romance and took charge:

"Hey Chief. Tina and I need a favor."

Belinda turned from the two Cupids she had just released for the Starbucks near Central Park West. She had a good feeling about the Forecast and admonished them both to take at least four True Love Arrows in their Quivers. Four is a lot, but Belinda had been doing this a long time. She could read Forecasts like most folks did introductory Soduko. In ink.

"No. You don't get your quivers back."

(both Tina and Burt turned a Pink that bordered on Red Rose)

Tina spoke first:

"We don't want our Quivers back (Belinda raised an eyebrow, and that look needed no words to accompany it) ...well (settling down to her usual light pink colored cheeks, and peaches toned body) we do, but that isn't why we came. "

"Well, what favor do you need?" Belinda said "Favor" with that: "I hear you, but I am not promising you anything tone," she was famous for. It was the tone that both Burt and Tina were hoping for. It meant Belinda was open to suggestions.

We need to get a your permission to order a "Chance Encounter."

Belinda's eyes widened, Chance encounters weren't rare, but uncommon. Most Humans ended up falling in Love with folks they knew well, or hung around a lot. A "Chance Encounter" well, that is the reason Humans made Romance Movies and wrote Romance Stories. Belinda had a secret passion for Human Romance Stories. She had quite the collection in her Aerie. They were sappy, and she cried over them, but they were delicious.

"What kind of Chance Encounter are you looking for?"

Tina looked at Burt and nodded. Burt took over:

"We want a Full Chance Encounter. With all the trimmings too!"

Belinda merely grunted, and waved them both to hover closer to her desk.

"You want a Full Chance Encounter? One with all the trimmings, like breathlessness, frozen moments of time, open souls, forgiveness, passion, and laughter?"

"Well, yes."

Belinda let out a long sigh, it came out like a soft summer wind and smelled of children playing on swing sets, and old people holding hands.

"You know the Department of Romance Chance Encounter Section is only allowed to grant those to Cupids who are certain that there is a True Love waiting to be born. They have never forgotten that Romeo and Juliet Fiasco when True Love was found too early because of some over eager Cupids with too many Arrows, and not enough experience."

Tina and Burt both let one shiny tear fall. All Cupids knew about the danger of True Love coming too early. Many Humans cannot survive losing their True Love at any age, but Teenage Angst, well, it makes it doubly hard to lose. Like all Cupids, Tina and Burt were shown the Arrows that were used on Romeo and Juliet. Scarbird (the Cupid who shot Romeo with True Love Arrows) gave the talk. It was his way of making sure it didn't happen again. Serene - well, she has never forgiven herself for firing her True Love Arrow into Juliet.

After a period of suffering and compassion, Serene was transferred to the Department of Mother's Love Section. She fits in there well. As those arrows are so soft, and can be fired as soon as the baby opens its eyes. Most Mother's hearts are open either with expectation, or simply because they are exhausted from the brutal ordeal that qualifies as being born for Humans. Either way, the arrows often land smack in the middle of Lifetime Unconditional Love. It has helped Serene heal.

*****

Belinda hovered quietly. Her wings caressing the air with just enough of a nudge to keep her stationary. She closed her eyes and

22

thought. Tina and Burt weren't consciously trying to hold their breath- but when Belinda opened her eyes again, they both inhaled again.

"Okay. Because of your track record...in the past. You know, before the Office Party. (Tina and Burt cringed. Will that ever be forgotten, or forgiven?) I am going to give you a slip for Edgar over in Chance Encounter. Tell him I said to give you a Full Chance Encounter...and...and... to add Mist.

Tina and Burt fell to the floor. They had forgotten to flap their wings for a second. Luckily, the whole Department had floors as soft as Cotton Candy, for just such awkward moments. It only took them a second to bounce right back, wings sparkling in overdrive (just picture a rainbow driven by a hurricane, it is a blur of pure beauty).

"You're going to give us Mist?

Belinda Nodded.

"Past or Future?" Asked Tina.

"Both."

Tina and Burt fell to the floor again. Which made a smile as big as Christmas morning break out on her face. When they fluttered to appear in front of her desk again she said in a quiet voice:

"You aren't the only two who have a good feeling about this. The Mist will allow them to judge this relationship on its own merits and not those of past loves. And it will also cloud their future enough so that they know they can have one, but they have to build it themselves. That is what Mist is for."

Tina couldn't help it, she buzzed right over and gave a very Cupid-like wet suction kiss right on Belinda's lips. It made Belinda turn that fiery pink that looks like Red Rose on most Cupids.

"Thank-you! Thank-you! Thank-You!" Cried Tina and Burt as if they were a choir practicing perfect harmony. Belinda waved them off:

"Shoo. Go over to the Chance Encounter Office before I change my mind." And she waved them away with her tiny perfect hands. Once they turned and soared off thru the Arch, Belinda reached up and rubbed her cheek with one hand- smiling at the memory. "Cupids," she thought to herself: "are so cute."

*****

The Chance encounter happened at a donut shop. He had been writing all morning on his Novel in that same quiet corner he always used. Just his laptop, some chocolate milk, a glaze donut, and time to think, that is all he ever needed. He had been in a hurry that day, and left his jacket with his smartphone hanging on the chair. He was already to 42nd Street when he realized he had left his jacket, with phone and wallet, hanging from that chair in the donut shop. He hurried.

*****

She saw the young man leave. He seemed distracted and that is what caught her eye. He was in a hurry that is for sure. That gave her enough time to study him some more. She had seen him once or twice before. Kind of a serious disheveled artists look. Clean though, not dirty and scraggly at all, like he did the basic hygiene things by rote, and not with any real purpose. He had a face that relaxed while he was thinking, and became all sharp lines, cut edges, and intent when he was writing. She liked that.

She looked back after he left the store. He had forgotten his coat! She knew she would never catch him. This is New York City at lunch time for crying out loud, by now he was just another faceless member of the throng of thousands hurtling through their daily life in Manhattan. He could be steps from the door and she wouldn't be able to see him.

So she decided to go babysit the coat. She figured he would come back eventually, and she had the time, a coffee, and a good book. She settled into his chair unaware of both the light lingering scent of his presence, and the male odor that made her snuggle up against the jacket. It was then that Tina unleashed the Mist.

******

Burt had impeccable timing. It is one of the things Tina liked most about working with him. He never let Cupid's Arrows fly too early, or too late. And he had the same knack for applying the Mist.

As the young man came hustling through the door, scanning the tables for his jacket, Burt waited until the woman waved at the almost out of breath young man. With a big smile, and one hand, she pointed to his jacket (still securely hanging behind her on the chair), with her other hand she waved him to join her. When they made eye contact...Burt let the Mist loose.

******

Tina and Burt flew back to Cupid Central. The Full Chance Encounter had worked! The Mist was doing its job. They had stayed and watched as the afternoon became late afternoon, and then early evening. And still the young man and woman sat talking together. Cups of hot chocolate and the crumbs of more than three donuts littered the table top as they chatted unaware of time, their surrounding, or what was happening to them.

Tina and Burt left the donut shop to fly back and tell Belinda about their success. A team would have to be assigned to let the Arrows of True Love fly, and they would have to be the Iron Hard True Love Forever Arrows that the Cupids used. If Tina and Burt were correct (and they thought they were) this love would be in the Top Three of all Time...if not the Number One Love ever.

So they were both caught by surprise when not only Belinda, but every Cupid from every Department was hovering in a giant mass of cuteness beyond comprehension in the lobby of Cupid

Central, the only place big enough to hold all their tiny bodies. Every one of the Cupids was beaming from ear to ear, and their combined breath smelled like a strawberry covered future in a giant bowl of the Milk of Human Kindness. It is the sweetest smell anyone could ever ask for.

A bit confused they floated up to Belinda whose face gave away nothing.

Without a word, Belinda pulled out both quivers from behind her back. Handing them to the stunned Tina and Burt. Who both fell to the floor, wings forgotten, as they held onto their quivers with all their might.

"You have got to stop doing that. We don't have enough people to clean the floor all day, and straighten out your wings too!"

With that Belinda smoothed a small kink out of Tina's left wing.

"But...but...but...why?" Tears, questions, and gratitude fell in equal proportions from both Burt and Tina.

"Because we just got a call from the Department of Chance Encounters. They told us that in the History of their Department, not one Chance Encounter has blossomed like this one. In fact, the Mist has infused itself into both Humans. And we didn't even know that was possible. They had already forgiven each other for anything that has happened, or anything that might happen.

In fact, HE called, and said: "I want Tina and Burt to shoot the Golden True Love Arrows. I think they have found real True Love. "

"HE called and said that?"

Belinda could only Nod. Nobody spoke with HIM, and was left unshaken. It took a couple of decades for all the joy to leak out.

With solemnity seldom seen among Cupids, The Head of Chance Encounters (Edgar) and Belinda handed one Golden Arrow of True Love to Tina, and the other to Burt.

"You only get one shot, don't miss."

Quivers slung over their shoulders, Burt and Tina flew up up up and out of Cupid Central. The humming of thousands of wings singing a love song only heard once or so in millennia. True Love had been found, and founded on a Chance Encounter.

******

"One…two…three." On Tina's command the Arrows of True Love flew simultaneously from their bows. The Young man and the young woman stopped talking and reached for each other's hands. And that is how they left the donut shop…hand in hand. It would be another seventy one years until they let go of each other.

A Chance Encounter. A True Love. And two Cupids got their quivers back.

Belinda turned to a "First Crush" request on her desk. Still smiling from the day's work. Without thinking her hand went to her cheek where hours earlier Tina had left her soft wet kiss- it was a good day to be a Cupid.

THE LETTER

By Kevin Hughes

"It's for you, Honey."

"Really? Who's it from?"

"I don't know. It is addressed to: Mrs. Sparkle Hauser (nee Kurtzweil)- so it must be from someone who knew you before you married me."

With that, Ben Hauser thought no more of it, and handed the letter to his wife. If he noticed how wide her eyes were, or that she seemed to have stopped breathing, and that her skin had gone almost as pale as the off white wall she was standing by- he sure didn't give any hint that he noticed. Instead, he took the Wall Street Journal and a catalogue for the Great Courses in his hand, laid the two bills on the small table in the foyer, and growled off to his study. The headline of the WSJ ringing in his body language- the letter to his wife, and his wife herself, already forgotten.

A part of Debbie "Sparkle" Kurtzweil - known as Mrs. Benard Hauser for the last forty four years- acknowledged that her husband wouldn't notice the intimate tone of the word "Sparkle". Nor would he connect it to her. It was mailed to her, not him, and therefore it was just some Women's gossip, or an old friend writing to her. Not his business. A part of her thanked him for his unconcern. Another part wondered what her life might have been like- had she not married an Engineer.

All that was cast aside like the remnants of a tidal pool when a fresh wave rushed in- but in this case, bringing in the old, not the new. For she recognized the handwriting, and the nickname. She hadn't seen the one in over four and half decades, and hadn't heard the other in five decades. It had to be from Brian.

She leaned up against the off white wall of the hallway, ironically enough, next to her High School Graduation picture. She was young, bubbly, vibrant, and joyful in that picture- her smile was huge, and meant for only one person to see- Brian. It was Brian that took that picture some fifty three years ago- and the only one she kept. All the pictures of her and Brian were tossed into the garbage the night she Married Ben.

"You don't keep memories of your past boyfriends or lovers when you get married. That's insane. Those people are not in your life for a reason. You are my wife now. Your old life is gone. Throw them all out. If you don't, I will."

She was only 23 at the time, young, naive, innocent- a newly Wedded Woman. Just a decade later she would have told Ben that her whole life counts, not just the time with him. But she was a young Bride. He was her future, she was in love, so to get along - she did as she was told. She didn't tell Ben that she kept one picture besides her graduation picture; that was the one her Brother Mike took of her and Brian.

31

Brian had just come home from overseas. He was wearing his Class A uniform with its newly minted Sergeants Stripes sewed precisely on both sleeves, his Service Medal placed right where they it was supposed to be: centered above the right pocket. He was proud of that medal, even though everyone got one just for being in the Army. He told her it wasn't like the ribbons, trophies, and awards that kids got for just showing up for sports nowadays. He said it told everyone that you served your country- and would have done anything they asked you to do.

It wasn't a "gimme" he said.

"It was... (and she remembered the fierce looking eyes when he told her): a token of having given up three years of your life to something bigger than yourself. Some gave up their lives because of that medal. It isn't a cheap bauble. It is a promise kept."

Mike had taken their picture just after Brian had made that little speech - and added one more sentence:

"Boy, Sparkle, I must have sounded like a pompous asshole there for a minute."

She laughed so hard she had to bury her head in Brian's Spotless Uniform, her tears of laughter moistening that very ribbon that the medal hung from. Brian's chin lay on top of her head (as it so often did when they danced, hugged, or talked), as one hand caressed her back in gentle loving circles, the other hand circling her waist to hold her safe against him. Brian was laughing too. And that was the moment her brother Mike caught for them. She kept that picture. She always would.

****

She hadn't even opened the Letter yet and memories started pounding up the stairs from the basement of her past. Bursting through the door of today like Cops in a Reality Show.

- Waiting at a red light outside Dairy Queen, when her ice cream cone fell onto the floorboard. Brian bent over to help her get it…a small "bang", "crunch", and two heads smacking into a handful of chocolate dipped ice-cream snapped back upright. Covered with ice cream, and little dignity, Brian apologized to the irate man who came to see who hit his car.

"What were you kids doing?"

"Eating Ice Cream."

"What?! (with incredulous dripping from that one word) on the floorboard?"

Brian had a wicked disarming smile as the told the man:

"Well my girl and I are both short, and the floorboard was closer than the dashboard."

How Brian said that with a straight face, she will never know. But she would never forget the face the man they hit had on his face. For his face literally corkscrewed from Anger and frustration, to outright hysterical laughter in just seconds.

- The time they fell asleep at the Drive-In theater. Waking up at 2 AM, unable to get past the unlocked chains to get out. Walking home from there took almost an hour and a half. Brian holding her hand the whole way, and telling her not to worry. She was so afraid that her parents would kill them both, or worse, make them break up. (A fleeting thought raced through her now seventy year old mind- a Smartphone would have really helped back then. It made her smile.)

When Brian rang the bell at my house. When my Dad and Mom both answered the door (they were both awake, worried, and mad as hell) Brian was ready. He told me later he had rehearsed his speech over and over on the long walk in the dark. Before they could say a word he said in a loud voice:

"Sparkle did nothing wrong. Neither did I. We just fell asleep in my car during the second movie. If you can't trust me, trust sparkle. She doesn't need to be yelled at, or questioned. We just walked three miles in the dark, she needs to go to sleep. So do I. So do both of you. Tomorrow, after School- we can talk about tonight - when we are all rested. Good-Night."

My parents never even got to yell. I went right to bed. They did too. On Monday, after school, Brian came over, and made us all laugh as he recounted our experience trying to pick the lock of the chain across the driveway. My Dad made us all laugh when Brian said:

34

"All the way home, Sparkle kept saying you would kill us both."

My Dad, deadpanned with a straight face:

"The thought had crossed my mind."

It was my Mother though that put us all on the floor:

"It crossed my mind too. It still is."

- When my best friend's Mother got sick, it was Brian who went over every night - for almost four months, to do chores, cut the grass, make dinner (Brian was one of the few boys I ever knew who could cook), do the laundry, and pack lunches for the next day. When she got better she told everyone that she finally had a son to go with her four daughters. I was so proud of him, and my best friend and I pitched in too.

The Memories were pouring in and out of her mind and heart- torrents of them, and still she hadn't opened the letter.

****

She went to her room. It was her arts and crafts room- Ben called it her "junk room". Brian would have called it her sanctuary. Brian would have been closer to the truth. She sat in her chair, turned on the old lamp, and sat back to read. She didn't get far before she sat back up straight- almost unseeing. She had read the opening sentence:

"Sparkle, I was afraid to write you for the longest time. Now that I am dead, it has to be safe to send this. I got Mike to promise to mail it when I died."

The letter fell to the floor, barely beating the tears that came unbidden, unwanted, unexpected, but necessary. It was a long time until she could pick the letter back up. When she finished the letter - long after Ben had gone to bed- she pulled out that picture her brother Mike had taken so long ago.

On the back of that picture, in the same chicken scribble penmanship of the letter she held in her other hand- Brian's handwriting- she read the short note:

"Young Love, True Love, Our love."

She turned the light out. Put the letter and picture in her private drawer and walked upstairs to where Ben lay sleeping. Wondering if forty years of marriage could match the meaning in that one letter. She went to sleep knowing the answer. She would read the letter again tomorrow.

And the next day.

And the next.

THE END

DEATH OF A BULLY

By Kevin Hughes

She didn't know what to say. So she didn't say anything. It made her life easier that way. She just couldn't think fast when someone was talking to her and if people were looking at her, she froze. She often dreamed of being invisible, and in those dreams she was able to to just go about her life without ever being noticed. But this time she was going to have to say something.

Why?

Because the big kid holding her purse for her wasn't going to be satisfied with just handing it back to her without at least a thank you. She was just gathering enough will power to actually speak to a stranger…a boy, no less, when she looked up and saw his eyes. She thought she was dreaming or something. Because those eyes were dreamy looking. A girl could get lost in eyes that looked like that. Especially if they were looking at her - and they were.

Whenever she was put on the spot, or stared at, or had to speak in front of the class, she got giant sweat stains under her armpits. That would make all the bullies laugh at her, both the male and the female kind. Even though her sweat didn't smell bad, the giant rings of sweat were hard to hide- so they earned her the nickname: Stinky.

As the big kid stared at her, she could feel herself sweating. That made her turn beet red. The sweat flowed from her armpits as if trying to see if it could imitate the amount of sweat road crews sweated in the sweltering sun in mid summer. Sweat that left salt rings on their shirts while working with hot asphalt.

The small circle of classmates who had gathered when that creep Dimassio had tripped her- didn't help ease the pressure either. First they all laughed at her- then they all stared at her; as the big kid quietly picked up all the things that had fallen out of her purse. He put all the things back in her purse and then extended his arm to hand her purse back.

And that is where they stood. Her looking up,a part of her not wanting to ever look away, and a larger part of her wishing she could just get away. Him standing a few feet away holding out her purse with one hand. It was then that she noticed what the big kid was holding in the other hand.

It was Dimassio.

****

At six foot one and one hundred and ninety five pounds, Dimassio was far from being easy to hold. Especially with just one hand. The Big Kid had a grip on Dimassio's wrist that was so strong you could almost see the bones grinding up against each other. Even if you couldn't see the bones grinding in Dimassio's wrist, you could see the pain and fear etched in his face. And the sweat pouring off of Dimassio's face wasn't sweet smelling either.

38

The Big kid just stood there, holding her purse- and the bully- with equal ease.

Still no one spoke. A few grunts of pain from Dimassio, some quick intakes of breath from those standing around, and a stage whispered: "Jesus, that kid is going to break Vince's wrist." Came from somewhere in the growing crowd. It looked more like a painting, with everyone holding still in just the right pose, than an actual event taking place in real time. She wanted to run. To hide. To become invisible. But something in the big kids green eyes held her in place.

Then it happened.

****

It was like a spell had been broken. Three things happened in quick succession. The bones in Dimassio's wrists gave out. You could hear both bones crack, like someone had just broken a branch over their knee to throw in a fire. That was the first thing.

Dimassio turned white- and fainted. Dead away. That was the second thing.

She found her voice AND stopped sweating too. That was the third thing.

All of those things were important. But they weren't the "it" that happened.

No. No. No.

This is the "it" that happened.

****

He was holding her purse by the strap. When she reached for her purse, their fingers touched. His eyes widened. Hers did too. Time stopped. But not their fingers. Her fingers climbed into his hand as if exploring for a place to settle in and stay put. His fingers found a way to link with each of hers and hug her palm close to his. The purse dangling, forgotten like yesterdays socks, no longer important to them, just hung like an ornament as it swung lightly under the two hands joining above it.

"I love you."

A part of her couldn't believe she said that. All of her agreed with it though.

"I love you too."

And all of him agreed with his answer.

The kids in the hallway broke into applause. Well, all but Dimassio, he merely whimpered as he wormed his way to the wall lockers to get in a sitting position. He looked up at the Big kid and she shy girl (Stinky) as hand in hand they turned and walked away.

"Lucky Bastard." Came out in a puff of pain from Dimassio's mouth.

"What?" Said one of his cronies reaching down to pull Vince to his feet.

"Lucky Bastards." (Nodding his head towards the couple with their backs to him)

"What…why?"

"Weren't you looking? They found True Love."

"But he broke your wrist!"

"So what? It was worth it to see that look."

"Why?"

"Because…you idiot, I want to recognize that look when I see someone give it to me. I know what to look for now. All it cost me was a broken wrist."

"Aren't you going to get even with him for breaking your wrist, or her for making a fool out of you?"

The look Dimassio gave his crony made that young man step back. The young man knew that look alright…it was determination.

"No. I am going to apologize to her. And thank him. They just showed me how to find that look. "

"How?"

"By being kind."

****

Six years later. The Big kid and Stinky had their first child. At the Christening the Godfather beamed with pride. Why wouldn't he? The child was named for him:

Vince.

The end

EPHEMERAL BLOOM

By Wess Luca

Life is fleeting. There are so many aspects of existence that barely have substance, and are then gone like vapors. Even the constants of life are always changing, like the weather. A chaotic hurricane contains an eerie stillness that belies the deadly intent of what is to come.

"What are you thinking about?" The masculine voice that assaulted Ariya's distracted mind jarred her out of her thoughts. She looked across the table and met the bemused expression of her companion.

"Hm?" Ariya asked with a dreamy and melodic tone. She understood his question, but was instead stalling for time. She had not the slightest idea of how to explain the direction her thoughts had taken, as their origins were part of her secret.

If one were to take a glance at Ariya where she sat at the outdoor café, they would almost certainly be inclined to take another as she was exceedingly beautiful. Dark hair that fell in buoyant ringlets framed her rounded face which carried a smattering of freckles dusted across her nose. The real reason for the second glance would be her eyes, however. Seemingly unnaturally green, Ariya's eyes could be compared to emeralds, in color and facet. Simply stated, she was unparalleled in human standards of beauty.

43

In spite of these features, Ariya was most certainly not human. Even an astute observer would not be able to tell the difference, unless they knew about the existence of the Fey. The Fey were an ancient race that at one point in history were known for beguiling the human race for their own whimsical lusts, but more recently have had considerably less prevalence.

The simple reason for the Fey losing infamy within the world of men is that they were dying out. When Fey intermingle with humans, they beget other humans. Only when Fey and Fey meet, can they have offspring of their own heritage. This would not be so difficult if their race did not have a full lifespan of only twenty years. A mere fraction of a life by the standards of men, but due to the whimsical nature of the Fey they often lived fuller lives than men could manage.

Even under the inquisitive stare of her friend, Ariya almost lost herself in thought again, but was saved by the repetition of the question.

"You seemed lost in thought." He explained, slowly leaning forward conspiratorially, for emphasis. "I was just wondering what you were thinking about."

This man who found himself in Ariya's company was actually quite handsome in his own right. His dark eyes might have contrasted her own, but were perfectly suited to his light brown hair that sat atop his softly squared head. Those eyes were constantly alit with energy and enthusiasm as if to make all present aware that he knew something they did not.

It was this playful nature that actually attracted Ariya to Ethan in the first place. His love for life mirrored her own, the only difference being that he possessed a much greater potential for it. Ariya had only known Ethan for a few months, but had decided not to tell him her secret for fear of spoiling the pleasant naïveté that so characterized him.

"I was just thinking about the weather." She said, deciding that the partial truth was better than no truth at all. His dark eyes pierced into hers, clearly expecting more than she had given, perhaps hoping to steal the truth from them.

"Yes, the weather is quite good today." He said when at last he found he could not pry anything from her expression. "Not a cloud in the sky. It would be a perfect day to explore the city." His eyes regained the sparkle that she thought to be his signature. This suggestion is exactly what a part of her had hoped would be the outcome of this day. Since Ariya had wandered into town and met Ethan, they had spent almost all their time having deep discussions and living out small adventures daily. She felt as though she had truly grown to love this young man.

The unfortunate fact of the matter was that the feelings were reciprocated. This was a problem that she often had, but one that humans rarely understood. At her current age Ariya was nearing the end of her lifespan, while Ethan was in his prime. For her to pursue anything with a human of his age would be reckless and irresponsible, which for any other Fey would not be a problem. She met his gaze evenly, still not resolute in her decision.

"And what have we left to explore?" She asked playfully, her indecision clearly reflected in her question. In fact, she found his mirth to be greatly desired because lately he had grown more withdrawn. It was slight, and others might not have noticed, but Ariya could tell and knew the cause. Almost a week prior the two had an exchange in which she stated her intent to leave soon. Ethan had not taken the news well, assuming her to be a more permanent fixture in his life.

"There is always more to explore." His eyes retained their sparkle, but there was a new edge to his voice. He waited a moment before continuing with new composure. "I feel as though you and I could continue to adventure every day and still not exhaust our options nor our spirits."

Though neither his eyes nor voice betrayed him, Ariya knew the profound sadness behind his plea, for she too felt it. He was indeed correct in what he spoke, but she knew that he took not her vitality into account, for what naive human would?

Every fiber of her being urged her to stay and live her final days in the bliss that she had grown to love, but she could not bring herself to do the selfish thing. She had experienced the rapid growth and unusually strong bond that they shared, and knew it would only grow as she lingered. She could see how Ethan would take the news of her unexpected death and how it would pierce him deeply. He would withdraw and lose much of his sense of adventure, perhaps his zeal for life. That was something that she could not allow herself to take from him.

Ariya looked deeply into his eyes and allowed herself to etch his expression into her memory until the pain was too great. It might be impossible for her to guard her heart any further, but she could do more for him. Newly resolute in her decision, she spoke with a firmness that she called from the depth of her conscience.

"No Ethan. I have cherished our time together more greatly than you can understand, but it has come to a close. Please know that I do not leave out of an emptiness of any kind, but rather that my heart dare not become any more full. Please do not ask me to stay, Ethan. Leaving is already more than I can bear." Ariya paused for a moment without meeting his gaze, then stood to leave.

"Wait, Ariya." Ethan spoke in a truly tormented voice, all pretenses of a facade dropped. Against her better judgement, she turned to regard him fully, taking in his pained expression all at once. Tears rimmed his eyes, threatening to spill over at the slightest provocation. He had also stood, but he seemed unsure of his action. He clearly wanted to beseech her to stay, but also desired to honor her request. Locked in place, his arm partially stretched out to her, he managed a single phrase.

"I love you."

Ariya looked at him squarely, her eyes now filling as well. She knew she had to walk away, or at least respond, but no strength came to her. It was as she at last opened her mouth to speak that the first raindrop fell upon her cheek. In the moments to follow the raindrops increased from sporadic to steady and soon they were both soaked through, holding each other's gaze.

"I cannot give you what you have given me. I have nothing to offer you. Goodbye, Ethan."

Before she could even finish her last words, Ariya turned and departed, knowing she had made the right decision. By leaving she had given him more than she could by staying. He could not afford to waste himself away on what he lost. Life is fleeting.

THE END

GEORGE, THE SINGING FROG

By Kevin Hughes

Ribbit, Ribbit, Ribbit...as the Frog goes....

It was a frog, not that much different than all the other frogs. Green, slightly slime covered, and horny and hungry a lot. What made this frog different from most is the simple discovery of its name: George.

George may be the first- maybe the only frog, to become aware of himself. His name was George. He liked the way it wrapped around his tongue. At night, when the males gathered to out croak their competitors- you could hear loud and deep "Ribbit, Ribbit...RIBBIT's" in a cacophony of sound. A sound that only sounded nice, if you were a green, slightly covered with slime, and frisky female frog.

Not George. He would yell his name out, and Frogs around him would grow quiet. A few of his former tadpole friends, would hop over and give him some pointers on how to "Ribbit Properly". Some would chide him. Other would shun him.

Still, despite their pointers, George would chirp out in a clear baritone: "George. George. George."

Late at night, way after all the frogs had left, George would remain at the pond.

"George. George. George." In his clear baritone voice would echo into the night.

He didn't know why he liked the sound of his name. He had never been particularly vain although he was once picked as the tadpole most likely to survive. He had an uncanny ability to find hiding places in the creek, the pond, and even a few on land. Even as an adult Frog, he never lost that ability. He hadn't seen all that many of his tadpole mates – since many of them didn't seem to have his ability. The few that did survive, well, ever since he started chanting "George" at the nightly pond dances- well, they came around less and less often.

Still, every night, George would go to the Pond: "George. George. George. " Getting better and better, experimenting with rhythm, time, and even tone. He could sing George better than any frog could Ribbit. Sometimes, the other frogs would stop to listen.

Not like they used to, out of shame, or disgust, but out of curiosity. Some, were not afraid to say: "I like the way he Ribbit's, it is very musical and pleasant to the ear."

Even some of the females talked to him. Frogs are very blunt creatures so they told him to his face:

"Your Ribbit's are strangely attractive. They make me want to just kind of nestle in the moss and listen. In fact, they often make me not want any company- male or female. I just want to listen."

Word got around. Soon, even snakes would gather around the pond. Snakes and frogs never got along before, and every frog was wary. But the snakes never even looked at the other frogs-nope. They just slithered into a tight curl, laid there with their heads   on   their   coils,   and   listened. "Sssssuperb….ssssssinging……Ssswonderfulll…" They wanted to tell George: "We like your singing George. But, of course, snakes cannot say: "George". Although many tried to, just so they could thank him for his singing.

Most of them figured out (correctly, I might add) that since they didn't eat George, or any of his fellows at the pond, that George knew they respected what he was doing. George did. The snakes frightened him at first, instinct, he thought. Yet, the snakes would always give him a smile before they slithered out of the forest floor near him. A gentle wave of their tale, as they uncoiled, and he could hear them say: " Sssooo longsss".

Soon more word got around. Deer came. Foxes came. Birds and even Owls (Owls! A Frogs' demon if ever there was one.). Still George played with his name. Adding echoes and reverb: "Thank God, for my air sack." thought George.

It got to the point that the senior frogs had to ask George not to Ribbit until after midnight. Ribbiting by other frogs had dropped to almost zero, since nobody Ribbit-ted- anymore when George was doing his thing. So George would stay in his log, or sometimes, under water, he would sit and think of how to expand his "George". At midnight, he would come out and try things.

Like the night he discovered he could use his giant back leg to beat on an empty log- and change the tempo. Speeding it up, slowing it down. Making it a chant, or even a ballad. Oh, and the other frogs delighted in that. They quickly caught on.

The drumming, in time, and always on the downbeat, caught the attention of the big animals too. Soon, the pond looked like a zoo after midnight.

Then one night, an amazing thing happened. All sound stopped. Not a single animal stirred, all of them holding their breath to see if what they thought they heard, they had actually heard. Even the owls, closed their eyes to listen harder.

Yes, there it was again; a strangely pleasing sound, much, much higher than the deep Ribbit's of George (since none of the animals were aware of their names- George was just a particularly fascinating Ribbit). This new Ribbit was very high, almost high enough for the songbirds to shake their heads and wonder: "Do we know her?" For it was definitely a her. The animals knew by the sound. George knew, because it was her name she "Ribbited" Into the night:

"Rita. Rita. Rita."

"GEORGE, GEORGE. GEORGE."

"Rita. Rita. Rita."

George hopped and splashed, and stepped on snakes, and even hopped over a fox in his hurry to find this "Rita." He looked up, over, around the pond - it was so big, where could she be? That is when the third biggest miracle George had ever seen in his life happened. An Owl, with its glowing yellow eyes, lifted a mighty wing, and pointed directly to the place where Rita stood. Rita froze in place, an owl pointing at you, right at you, has frozen many a frog- and often was the last thing a frog ever saw.

Not tonight though. The owl was like all the other animals in the forest. The owl did not want to lose George and his strange Ribbits. He pointed to the female, hoping that George would find her and together sing those strange appealing Ribbits for them all. Later, George would do exactly that. Right now though, he skidded in the soft mud at the feet of Rita. The owls pointing had brought him right to her.

He stared for a second; the shyest and most hopeful "George" he ever Ribbited, ribbited out. It was so full of emotion that a snake had to ask a rabbit to wipe its eyes for it. The Rabbit, never taking his eyes off of the scene of George meeting Rita for the first time- simply took his foot, and offered it to the snake. Neither knowing how lucky that was.

Rita was weeping. "He knows his name! Like I do. I am not alone." Trying to hold back her emotions, and to George's delight, failing miserably; Rita ribbited her name. It was a Ribbit filled with: longing, loneliness at an end, joy beyond belief. If they had not been frogs, it might even have been the sound of a prayer being answered.

George and Rita Ribbitted all through the night. There was no leaving the pond that night. In fact, all the animals stayed up to listen as George and Rita, found harmony, melody, and each other. Animals with fur, nuzzled without speaking. Those with paws gently placed them on the nearest member of their species. Even the snakes, coiled in huge mounds, tails gently locked, or draped over another, or maybe others.

The owls, well, they flew to stand by other owls. The pond had never seen a night like this. A night that changed everything, and nothing would ever be the same. Enemies became friends, friends became true friends, and love crossed over the huge divide separating amphibians from reptiles, and all of them from mammals.

That night, the only sounds were the rising and falling scales of the two ribbits: "George"- "Rita", as their hearts played, and their legs gently tapped out the time, the beasts and fowls of the jungle sat side by side, in what became a Garden. George and Rita, had made the pond into an Eden.

The end

FRIENDS AND FATE

By Tom Di Roma

"I think I might have found the perfect girl for you," Charlie said as I stuffed my laptop into my backpack.

I glanced sideways at him. "I've heard that one before."

"No, it's not like that. She's not looking for a date. She wants someone to help her with her writing."

Once again, I raised my eyebrows at him. "I think you may be barking up the wrong side of the tree with that one. I can barely fix my own writing, let alone try and fix someone elses. That's one of the reasons I'm going to this conference." It was going to be a four day affair at a hotel complex about two hours away.

"Well, you can at least call her up, can't you?"

I narrowed my eyes. "You're sounding awfully desperate all of a sudden. What's up?"

Charlie refused to look at me directly. "Well, you see," he said hesitanly, "I hear she's really, really cute, so I figured, if you help with her writing, and I happen to come along with you —"

"Then maybe she'd fall for you," I finished for him. Charlie nodded. "How did you find out about her, anyway?"

"She's the sister of someone at work." Then after a moment of silence, he asked, "So what do you say?"

I sighed. "Yeah, okay, after I get back from the conference, you can give me her number and we'll go from there."

Charlie beamed. "Great!"

Suddenly, a car horn blared outside. "That's my ride," I told Charlie and headed for the door. Charlie followed me. "I left you a beer in the fridge," I told him. "Lock up for me when you leave, will you?" Charlie had a key to my place. Not only had we grown up together, we were bowling buddies.

Since my car was in the shop, I had to find a ride to the conference. Luckily, the original ad listed a couple of people who wouldn't mind giving someone a ride as long as they paid for gas and food. My chaufeurs turned out to be a brother and sister duo—Brad and Cindy Cohen.

I sat in the back while Brad and Cindy took turns driving. It took us three hours instead of two. Really slow traffic. Once we got there, all three of us went straight to the pre-conference coctail hour. That's where I met Bonny.

A really cute, twenty-something looking brunette, she was standing next to the Hors d'oeuvre table talking to a much older dude. Watching them, I wished it was me she was talking to, but I knew that probably would never happen—not the way I looked.

Where Charlie was your typical handsome jock type, I was the short, slightly soft-looking nerd with glasses. But the one thing I was proud of was my writing, even though I hadn't had anything published yet.

Heading for the Hors d'oeuvre table, I decided to hover near the girl and the older dude and pretend I wasn't listen in on their conversation. But that's when I heard her say, "I'm mostly into science fiction and fantasy type stories."

My enthusiasm got the better of me, which was the reason I blurted out without thinking, "So am I!" Both turned to look at me.

I was just about to excuse myself for bothering them when I saw the girl's eyes light up. Did that mean she was interested in what I might have to say? Evidently she was, because she said with undisguised enthusiasm, "Oh, yeah! Who are your favorite authors?"

I stared at her a little dumbfounded. No one that pretty had ever said anything like that to me. Thinking fast, I rattled off several names.

"Wow!" she exclaimed. "We like the same authors!"

From then on, our conversation continued with the both of us talking about which stories from which authors we liked the best. In fact, we were so focused on each other's interest, we didn't even realize the old dude had slipped away.

From the coctail hour, everyone headed for one of the hotel's autitoriums where a famous mystery author was giving a keynote speech. Bonny sat next to me as we listened intently. Then I did something I would not normally have done—I asked her if she wanted to join me for supper. When she said yes, I became so deleriously happy, you could have knocked me over with the swish of a feather.

Reluctanly, I left her behind so I could check in at the front desk and then, after retrieving my backpack from the car, headed to my room. After unpacking most of my stuff, I rested a while then went to meet Bonny at one of the hotel restaurants for dinner.

It was like we were never separated; our conversation picked up almost exactly where it had left off earlier. After supper, we took a short walk around the hotel complex. That's when I found out a little more about her.

Like me, she was in her mid twenties. Unlike me, she was still living with her parents. She said it helped her to stay focused on her writing instead of going out and partying all the time. At the moment, she was working as a receptionist for an electronic's firm.

Then came "my question" to her. What did her boyfriend think of her writing?

She hesitated before answering. "I don't have a boyfriend . . . at least not at the moment."

"Why not?" I asked, not realizing I might have been digging a little too deeply into her personal life.

"Well, I did have one for a while, but we broke up." She became quiet before asking me, "Do you know what it's like trying to talk with someone about your writing and seeing their eyes glaze over?"

"Actually, I do."

Bonny went on to explain. "We got along great most of the time, but when it came to my writing, he was clueless."

Later after we separated, we met once again in the hotel bar area so we could exchange a short story each of us had brought with us. We had decided to look over the other's story and say what we thought about it. This could be dangerous, which was why I said to her, "You can be as rough on me as you want. I'm a big boy; I can take it."

"Me too," she said, but her eyes didn't reach mine. And so we took each other's story back to our rooms to read over and make notes.

The next morning, we met for breakfast in the same restaurant as the night before. That's when the fireworks began. Well, maybe not fireworks exactly, but there was definitely some tension.

If an author tells you he or she doesn't mind what you say about their story, they're lying. They do care. They want you to say you loved it. So when she started looking over my notes, I could immediately see she was getting upset, so I jumped in. "Now, you have to understand something," I said right away. "These are only my first impressions, so a lot of what I said might be wrong. With my own stories, it takes me several readings and several drafts before I'm satisfied with what I've written." She still didn't look at me directly. That's when I added. "Even with what I said, I really liked your story. You have a great way with words."

Finally, she smiled. "Thanks," she said. Then asked, "Aren't you going to see what I said about your story?" I hadn't opened the envelope containing my story yet.

I waved away her question. "I'll do it later. Right now, what do you want for breakfast?" I was hoping our little confrontation had not spoiled our budding friendship.

I was wrong, because that's when she said, "You know what? My stomach has been bothering me all night. I think I'll skip breakfast for now and maybe have something a little later." Then I watched her get up from the table and take her stuff with her. I felt like a boat dead in the water. All my hopes for continuing with our friendship had been dashed.

The rest of the conference, we pretty much kind of avoided each other, even though we were in the same group of writers who were trying to produce science fiction and fantasy stuff. But then on the last day, she approached me.

"I'm sorry I got so upset with you," she said, her eyes focused on my sweater instead of on my face.

"No problem," I told her. "Besides, you really are a good writer; everyone in our group thought so." That brought a little smile to her lips.

Each day our little group of fantasy scribes had been given assignments by our instructor to come up with something we could read and talk about the next day. Bonny got way more compliments on her stuff than I did. "So are we still friends?" I asked her.

This time, she did look up at me and smiled. "Friends," she replied, shaking my hand. That's when I gave her my name and number. I had been hoping we could become friends again. She surprised me with a slip of her own. Obviously, she had been thinking the same thing.

All the way home, I kept thinking about Bonny, and how I never would have met her had I not gone to the conference. Plus there was the fact she lived only two towns away from me.

We both promised to keep in touch. I got a thrill just thinking about it. And then the first time I saw Charlie, he said he had something to give me. "It's that girl's name and telephone number I was telling you about."

When I looked at the slip of paper he handed me, I barked out a laugh. Confused, he asked, "What's the matter?" That's when I told him about Bonny. "You mean, you spent four whole days with her!"

"Yep!" Of course, I wasn't going to tell him about our disagreement.

"Did you . . .?" he pumped his fist in an obsene manner.

I frowned. "NO! This was a writing conference, not a trip to Club Med!"

"But still . . ."

"Cut it out!" I scolded him.

"So when are you going to see her again?"

"I'll call her tonight and see if she wants to meet us at Scarpino's?" That was Charlie and I's favorite Italian restaurant.

He beamed. "Great! Let me know what she says."

"I will."

But things didn't go quite as Charlie had planned. It turned out Bonny had forgiven me, and even brought other stories for me to look over and comment on. It didn't take Charlie long to figure out she wasn't interested in him and so he stopped coming along when Bonny and I would get together.

Eventually, Bonny and I became more than just writing buddies . . .

But that's another story for another time.

THE END

SCRUNCH, BOOTS, AND A KITTEN NAMED EAGER

By Kevin Hughes

She could hear the kitten. It was meowing so loudly that even in the thick brush she could hear it clearly. The sound seemed to be coming from a small hollow under a thick elderberry shrub. She got on her hands and knees to look down into a hollow that was both deeper and darker than she had supposed. A pair of eyes looked back at her.

She couldn't help it. She twisted, squirmed, squiggled; crawling towards the small mound of dark fur with the big eyes. Edging a little farther into the hollow she heard a cracking sound, felt a thud against the back of her legs, and instinctively curled into a ball- all scrunched up. A moment later and the path behind her was closed off by a limb that must weigh more than a bus, or her whole house.

The kitten scrambled up to her and started licking her face. Even in the dark, all scrunched up, she had her arms free enough to cuddle the kitten, which was trembling as it licked her face and eyes. She couldn't help it, even in her present predicament (which her mind hadn't fully processed yet) she smiled as the kitten responded to the pressure of her arms by settling in and purring loudly.

"Well, aren't you eager to find a home, little kitty? Hmm. You know, I think I shall call you: "Eager." Yes. That suits you fine."

Eager responded with a gentle caress of her tongue- and a steady purr.

Before her mind could switch back to what she might do next, she saw through a small gap a shaft of light. The light was blocked. She heard some grunting, some more grunting, and then a stick made the gap a bit wider. Looking behind her from inside the hollow, she could make out a pair of boots. Fine boots they were too, made out of some fancy purple leather, and wound with gold laces.

"Great. I am trapped in a hollow cave by a tree or a rock of some kind, and I get a Court Dandy to rescue me." She laughed. The kitten stopped purring to peer at her in the dim light- as if to say: "Are you okay?" She was. Even if the Dandy was a complete fool, he would summon help to get me out of here- at least that is the way her thoughts led her.

"Hello in there! Are you okay?"

"I'm fine. I just can't move forward, and something is blocking my way out. Oh, and I have a kitten."

She had no idea why she added that last bit, but the gentle laugh that came out of the small opening behind her nestled in her heart the way the kitten had found her arms. Her heart grasped it with the same eagerness she found in the kitten.

"Oh, well, then. That certainly makes it worth your while to be half buried in a den on a deserted hillside."

There was no rebuff in his voice, no hidden judgment call. Nope. Just solid good humor suggesting he might have done the same thing she did, had he heard the call of the kitten.

"I don't mean to be rude, but all I can see are your boots. Can you get me out of here? I mean, by yourself, or do you have to go get help?"

"Well, most of a giant Elm tree is in the way. I am quite strong for my thin frame, but I couldn't get it to budge. However (he went on before her hopes could sink lower) I am a fair hand with a shovel, or stick, so I shall just keep digging until you can squirm back out. Don't panic, it might take me a while since I don't have the shovel, just a stick."

"I won't panic. It might scare the kitten!"

His laugh came back through the small opening like a dollop of hope that quickly found a spot in her heart to take root next to the earlier laugh. She heard the constant scrape, scrape, scrape, and then the follow up, brush, brush, brush, as he dug out some dirt and rocks, pulled them out with his arms and hands, and started in again.

She couldn't see what he was doing, and without being told, she knew to keep her eyes closed in case anything fell in on her- but she knew he was working fast- and hard. She wondered why he was hurrying.

Outside the small den blocked by the giant fallen tree, the young man in purple boots kept one eye on the giant trunk. He had seen it shift a few times. He knew if it rolled over onto the girl (he thought it was a girl) trapped in there, she would be crushed. And the kitten she went to save too. He didn't let his fear take control, but he did let it loose to fuel his muscles to dig in even strong strokes. He knew he was in a race against time...or death.

There was light enough to see now. Even the kitten had turned in her arms to look back over her body to see what was going on. She couldn't move her shoulders out of the way to look back any farther than she had before he started digging for real. So she just relaxed and watched the kittens face.

She felt two strong hands grab her ankles without warning. She yelped. The kitten dug its claws into either side of her face as her grip tightened. Then she was flung a good six feet through the air as she sailed by and looked down at a delightful looking young man with a look of surprise on his face - it made her smile. She hit the hillside with a grunt, but that glimpse of her rescuer was still plastered on her face. For her face lit up when she saw his, and she saw the reflected light in his.

Then she saw the boots again. Then a hand reaching to help her up. Even after she was standing, her head had to continue looking up...and up...and up. This was no boy, this was a man. Granted he may have just become one in the last season or so, but there was no doubt that he was a man. No boy could be that tall, that wide, that lanky, and that confident. He must have been six and a half feet tall, and his hands were the size of the shovel he didn't have.

She looked down at the hole he had dug in just a few minutes, with nothing but his hands and a stick the size of a wooden mixing spoon. Then she saw the size of the tree trunk - and whistled.

"I could have been crushed!"

"My thoughts exactly."

They both laughed so hard, they had to lean against each other to catch their breath. The kitten, caught between two humans, let out a little growl that made them pull apart, but not much. The look the kitten gave both of them, set them to giggling again. The kitten climbed up onto her shoulder, allowing the two young humans to close the gap in their embrace - again. After a bit, her head nestled into his chest - she told him how she ended up in there.

He listened. Then told her he had seen her from the trail he was on, and was coming over to introduce himself when she bent down and disappeared. Then he heard the tree snap and fall. He thought she was dead, but he heard the kitten and her talking. So he dug a little hole under the trunk, saw that she was scrunched up in a ball. The rest of the story, they both knew.

"I only saw your boots. So I shall call you Boots (blushing furiously) but only when we are alone. "

He blushed back in complete agreement.

"I shall call you Scrunch. As that is all I saw of you- at first."

"I named the kitten: Eager."

He smiled that giant gentle smile she grew to know so well.

"You could have named me that too, once I saw you."

"Sorry Boots, but he got the name first, but if it helps, I am eager to know more about you."

"Well, then I am eager to get Eager home, and eager to know more about you too."

With the kitten in one arm cupped and cuddled, her free hand was locked in his giant hand. The dirt and soil still covering his hands unnoticed by either her or him.

And so it was, that the legend of Scrunch and Boots was born. A couple so deeply in love that their private names became their only names. Seventy four years of marriage never once dimmed the kindness and humor they shared. A series of cats, all named "Eager" made their life long journey with them.

Their tombstone had no last name, no dates with dashes- just this:

Boots and Scrunch

Forever.

A stone kitten wearing a tag that said: "Eager" perched on the top of the Marble slab.

Legend has it that if you pass a hollow under a tree, you can hear a kitten, and laughter from a couple too. Boots and Scrunch.

The end

COSMIC CONNECTION

By Tom Di Roma

There's a cosmic connection between some people. Usually we say the two people involved are soulmates, that they were destined to be together. Of course, neither we nor they know it's going to happen until it does. But on some rare occasions, the connection is felt by one, or both parties, though they may not know what they're experiencing. All they know or sense is that there is someone or something out there waiting for them. Such was the case of Lilly and Nick.

Both were musicians. She played the cello in an orchestra, while he played the guitar and sang in his brother's band. Neither knew of the other's existence, and yet somehow when each played they could almost hear the other's song.

Lilly was living in New York City at the time, while Nick was in Los Angeles playing a steady gig with his band in a newly renovated nightclub.

One day they both decided to write a song for themselves. They began by putting pen to paper. But what would have blown each of their minds had they found out was the fact that the notes for each song were exactly the same, which was the reason they could almost hear, in the back of their minds, an echo of the song being sung or played from afar.

At night, each would lay in bed listening to the other's song, but neither told their fellow musicians. They knew their mental health would be called into question, so each kept the secret to themselves.

It wasn't until they both began to tour that the other's music began to filter more strongly into their consciousness's. This was when a sense of desperation began to grow in both—it was a desperation to find out where the music was coming from.

Lilly began to search first. She and her orchestra were in Phoenix. Because she knew that the echo of her song was being played by someone with a guitar in a rock band, she began to check out several bars where rock bands were playing. At the same time, Nick began to hit places where orchestras could be found.

Finally, on the last night for both, they discovered each other in the park near Lilly's hotel. She had heard an acoustic guitar playing her song in the park below her balcony. With great excitement, she took her cello down to the park and began to play along with the guitar.

"Oh, it's you!" said Nick with breathless wonder when he saw and heard Lilly playing their song. "But how . . .?"

Stopping a moment, Lilly just shrugged. "We must be connected by the universe." Then she once again began to play their song in tandem with his guitar. Their music became like a synchronized dance, each note flowing smoothly alongside its twin. They continued to play for almost an hour. Then they walked back to her hotel room and made sweet love, not speaking, not promising anything. Their music and each other was all they needed.

It wasn't until the next morning that they talked about who they were and what they wanted out of life. Lilly wanted to become one of best cellists around. Nick just wanted to continue to play rock with his brother and their band. Just before they separated, each gave the other contact information, then they parted with a deeply felt kiss.

A month later, Lilly discovered she was pregnant. She didn't tell Nick; she didn't think she needed to even though both had talked a lot on the phone since that night.

Seven months later, Nick and Lilly ended up in the same city, and that's when Nick found out about Lilly's condition. He didn't have to ask if it was his; he'd been having strange dreams. In his dreams, he'd seen Lilly holding and nursing a baby boy. Never once while on the phone did he ask her about it—he was too afraid. But now, they discussed about what to do. Nick wanted to quit his band and just stay with Lilly until the baby was born, but she wouldn't let him. She decided he should continue to tour with his band, and then she would contact him once the baby arrived, which she did.

At that point, both quit their respective situations, taking up residence in a house that Lilly had inherited from her late mother. Together, they raised their son, whom they called August, for the month in which he was born. Lilly taught music to struggling adolescents, while Nick played in local bands. What they didn't know at first, but discovered very quickly, was that they had produced a musical prodigy. August was writing music and playing the guitar by the time he was four. Eventually he joined several garage bands until he was old enough to play in clubs.

Both his parents were extremely proud of him. They became even more so when he joined a major rock band and began to tour. But then one night Lilly received a strange phone call from her son. He told her he could hear music at night while lying in bed. "It's soothing and helps put me to sleep, but I don't know where it's coming from!"

Lilly smiled knowing exactly what was going on. That's when she told him about how she and Nick had come to be a couple. It was something she had never told him before.

"So what do I do about it?" he asked her.

"Just lay there and enjoy it. It's your soulmate calling to you. Let the music wash over you, and then one day, you and her will find each other without even trying."

So that's what August did. And eventually, he met Amber. She was a violinist in an orchestra. Together, they produced August Jr. And he too followed in his parent's footsteps.

THE END

GUITAR MAN

By Kevin Hughes

The notes hung in the air. Some shimmering a bright metallic silver. Other notes, more perfect and less slippery, shone gold. The song itself was nestled in all the strings with the wrapping of warm wood as a cover. He didn't sing. He didn't have to. The guitar sang it all.

He never spoke much. When he did, his voice came out rough, rippled, raw, like he hadn't used it in a while. He never spoke on stage. Except at the end of the night when everyone in the place he was playing would stand, overcome with the music. He would absorb their emotions- then say: "I thank you." It was enough.

She saw him first, in an alley. She had to come back to see if it was just a lumpy pile of rags or trash. Part of her thought it could be a man, and that part turned out to be right. The pile of broken and bloody rags moaned. She knelt to turn the pile over- blood dribbled from his mouth, his nose was flattened, turned to one side of his swollen face. A face that looked like someone had carved it into a pumpkin, then- smashed it with a hammer.

Blood and snot bubbled out of what she barely recognized as a mouth:

"Is my guitar okay?"

She had no idea what he was talking about. He must have taken to many blows to the head and is just spouting nonsense-she thought. She was wrong.

He lifted a quivering hand to her face, turning her cheek (now covered with gore and blood from his swollen palm) with the one eye that could open enough to see, he looked right at her:

"Is my guitar okay?"

She heard the anguish in that voice. She had heard it in her own voice when her husband died (and she had not) in that terrible crash. She knew the pain, worry, and fear behind the question. Hers had been: "Is my husband okay?" His was: "Is my guitar okay?" It was the same question. She looked around hoping beyond hope that she could give him a better answer than she had gotten.

There, sitting on top of some barrels was a guitar case. It didn't look beaten or broken like he did. Just battered from the dings and dangs of long use. She rose from his side and pulled it off the barrels. Bringing it to where he could see the case.

"Open it, please."

Came out in a puff of blood snot, snort of pain, and hope.

She fumbled in the dark, releasing the catches. Inside was a well cared for, obviously well used, guitar. Old. Certainly. But not broken, bent, or wrecked.

His one good eye shed a single tear. Glistening with thankfulness that eye turned towards her:

"You can get me help now. If you please."

That too came out with bubbles of bloody goo from his weirdly angled jaw. It must have taken all his strength. Because as soon as he said it, he passed out. She flipped out her cell phone and called for help. The whole time until the ambulance got there, she sang to him the same songs her mother used to sing to her when she was sick.

She didn't know if he could hear her (he did). She didn't know if it was helping (it was). She didn't even know if he wanted to live. (he did) She did know she had to sing. (so did he) So she sang…and sang…and sang.

****

Months in the hospital, several surgeries, and two major infections later- the Guitar Man was released. The men who beat him because they thought his music was directed at their girlfriends, found that their jealousy put them in jail longer than the Guitar man was in the hospital. With release a mere imaginary date years and years away. The guitar man remembered little about that night. He never saw the first blow from the pipe coming. After a few more blows, he didn't even feel the blows themselves.

All he remembered was an Angel singing, telling him is guitar was okay.

****

He had no way to thank the Hospital Staff. He asked if they would all come to the picnic table out behind the Hospital. A pretty little patch of nature set behind the big building held that picnic table, was only for Staff, and the few long term patients (like he had been) to enjoy some solitude under the trees next to the small river that ran down the valley. They knew he loved that guitar- the lady who brought him to the Hospital said to keep it near him.

"Let him see it when he is healing. It means a lot to him. I think it is like Family to him, or maybe like a True Love. Don't take it away from him. It is the only thing he asked about until the Ambulance got there."

So that is what they did. He didn't regain consciousness for those first few days. When he did float up to the barest level of human thought, he looked over and saw his guitar case on the chair. He smiled. Drifted right back down into the darkness, but this time feeling safer. The Nurse noted it in the recovery log. They kept that guitar near him - always.

****

They all sat around the picnic table as the guitar man tuned his guitar. None of them had ever heard him play. Only two of the night nurses ever saw him gently stroking the strings late into the night and early morning. His fingers moving in the softest caresses over those strings. Barely bringing out any music that could be heard more than a few inches away. It seemed so intimate that it embarrassed both nurses that they even watched. They never told anyone. Nor did they try to look in on him again when he held his guitar.

Fifty different Staff: Doctors, Nurses, Surgeons, Orderlies, Cooks, even the cleaning crew were gathered. Each holding the little hand drawn (with great care)invitations the had made for them. Each just a little different than the others- all strangely beautiful in a way. Everyone kept their invitations after showing them to the Guards- for this was a private affair, the invitation was a true gift for each of them.

He had tuned his guitar several times. He was ready. But there was still one invitation that hadn't shown up. He would wait a few more minutes. If that invitation didn't show. Then he would begin. If that invitation did show, he would talk for the first time in months. Everyone seemed to sense something was holding him back-for they grew quietly curious, not restless.

****

She showed the guard her invitation. She had no idea why he had sent her one. All she did was sing to him until the ambulance got there. She rode in the back with him, the paramedics, and his guitar. When they rushed him straight to surgery- she told the Head Nurse about the incident with the guitar. The Nurse was ready to blow his words off as the ramblings of a severely concussed man- which he obviously was. Something in the way the woman spoke when she handed the battered guitar case to the Nurse, warned her that this person meant what she said:

"You keep that guitar where he can see it, if he wakes up."

The Nurse did just that.

She didn't think that warranted an invitation to his recovery party. He did.

****

He looked up. It was her. He knew it. She was looking around shyly at the gaggle of doctors, nurses, hospital staff, wondering why she was even there. He smiled. It was that smile that made everyone turn and look at what, or who, made him smile like that. She didn't see the smile at first, she only felt it. It made her turn.

She saw him for the first time. A tall rugged looking man. A bit pale, like he had just come out of a long convalescence (which, indeed, he had…just). Broad shoulders, long slender hands, and a face that belonged out West. His face and jaw were set like canyon walls, and his nose- strangely enough- looked like a out of place gully down the middle of those stone like cheek bones. It didn't make him look ugly, or handsome, merely solid. But the smile.

That smile looked like someone carved joy, hope, love, dreams, and the future into rainbow shafts of light coming out of the cliff sides of his face. It was the prettiest smile she had ever seen. But then, she couldn't see her answering smile, which matched his in both power and rainbow shafts. He did.

****

He motioned her up to the picnic table. One of his long arms reached out to take her hand in hers. For a long moment everyone watched as whatever happened between those two…grew. Some Nurses sighed. Some cried. One of the Doctors texted his wife and daughters: "I love you." Another leaned over and hugged the Nurse next to him whispering: "I never told you. But I have loved you since you started working with me two years ago." Without taking her eyes off of the two at the picnic table, she leaned back into the Doctor whispering in her ear: "I know. Me too."

For whatever was happening at the picnic table was rippling through the hearts and minds of everyone there.

The moment didn't fade, as much as just step back for a bit. He released her hand, strummed golden notes with promise of more to come with one test of the strings. And then he spoke:

"Would you sing, if I play?"

She merely nodded. She had no idea what he would play.

His fingers moved. The guitar sang. Notes came back to echo bloody snot bubbling away air and life from a battered body.

Pain. Pathos. Longing. And then…notes of hope. Notes the carried the future into the present. She recognized those notes. They were the songs she sang to him on that blood pooled dank alley floor. She knew he had heard her. She knew her songs saved him. She knew his music would saver her. So she sang.

He played. She sang. Everyone listened. Everyone loved.

He was the guitar man. She was his singer.

The end

THE CROOKED ROAD

By Kevin Hughes

Author's Note: Even though this is a work of fiction. Many of the crooked paths are taken from real life. No one knows the crooked road their life will take to lead them to the ones they love. If you don't believe me, look back at your five year old self and see if that child would have believed any of the things you eventually did. After all, you can drive a car! Here is the story with bits of truth intertwined in the Fantasy.

It was their first night together- in the hospital.

Because of their ages: she was 91 and he was 94, they put them together in the same room. As their Doctor told the Nurses:

"They have been together for seventy one years without spending a single night apart. I am not going to be the one to end that streak."

All of the Nurses agreed.

When the Nurse at the Assisted Living community found her curled around her husband, after both of them had gone missing from both breakfast and lunch- the Nurse knew it wouldn't be long for him...and his wife would follow soon of a broken heart. So they were sent to the hospital, as they always were, and always would be- together; a couple. The Hospital agreed with both the Nurse from the Assisted Living Home, and their Doctor. They would share a room until the end.

And so it came to pass that the couple found themselves holding hands in the middle of the night, just as they had for decades.

"Kevin. Kevin, are you asleep?"

"I was."

The quiet laugh was so much a part of their routine now- that it brought on a second wave of laughter. Soft laughter though, for neither had much breath, and neither wanted to disturb the warmth of darkness. She stopped laughing to say:

"I was just thinking…"

"About what, Honey?"

"About how strange it was that we met. How long of a time we have had together. What a crooked road we took."

The silence was one of thoughtfulness, filled with recollection that searched back through almost a century. It was several minutes before he spoke:

"I know honey. A girl from rural Canada, one of eight siblings, who stood in a Farmer's field at five years of age, sniffing her arm to smell the sun on it, had no clue that she would meet someone from another Country - and marry him."

"I know that darling. A six year old boy from the inner city in a Midwestern Steel Town, sat on the stoop of an old house, making small mounds of dirt into hills for his Army Men to attack. A boy who used old cigarette filters soaked in lighter fluid to make the battlefield look bombed out and real, had no idea he would meet a Farm girl from Canada. His ten siblings were as surprised as he when he found her."

The two frail hands with paper thin skin, rustled against each other in the darkness, like parchment being carefully flipped over to read the other side.

"You know, darling, I think that the crooked road started there, in our childhood. A road that took you to college- the first of you family to ever go. Then to a Church Mission that sent you to a different country - to a small town in the middle of nowhere. Then...to me."

Their grip on each other hands, though not as strong as it used to be, was still powerful enough to lay unbroken by either.

"I agree, honey. For you left those tiny steps to go to the Army, see half the world, only to be refused another tour in Hawaii. You decided to go to College in Texas. When you saw me and my Companions moving into an apartment, you just came over and started helping us carry stuff. You didn't belong to any Church, and didn't want to. Yet we met."

"That didn't make your Mom to happy."

The laughter that came then was the healed laughter that had to be strong enough to overcome the pain and length of time it took make people who weren't in love, recognize that those two were in love. Family tried to tear them apart long before Family understood. The could laugh about it now, and did.

"Your Mom told me that I was so special, I could do better than you,Kevin."

He laughed heartily at that. For he knew that it was a true story. And it made her laugh that he always agreed with him Mother. His Mom considered his wife, her daughter, or at least another one of her daughters.

Time drifted by again, as the crooked road took them on slightly different paths, the In-Law path was different for both of them. But at the end, their love had not only united them, but two families too.

His laugh started up again, this time she could feel the absolute joy echoing in it. It was the kind of laugh that brought the word "Funny" to life. So she asked what was so funny?

"Remember our Wedding night?'

Now her laugh echoed hers. The tears had to be wiped away with her free hand, and she reached across his chest to dry his face too. They laughed in that half hug, half caress position for many moments.

"I sure do." Came the muffled reply, as that interaction played itself out in both their minds. "But tell me again what we said."

His smile would have lit up a much bigger room, dispelling any darkness at all.

"You came out of the bathroom in that flimsy transparent night gown. Your body was young, filled with curves and anticipation. I was so turned on I could hardly breathe. You stopped at the foot of the bed, turned beat red (everywhere- I could see) then said:

"Kevin. I am a virgin."

I said: "I am too."

To which you said: "Well this is going to suck."

The peals of laughter made the Night Nurse peek in on them. Two old people snorting and laughing while snuggled. She thought it was cute and just quietly closed the door. They never even knew she had peeked in on them.

The night wore on. The jobs they had to endure, the children they had, the times that they were homeless early in their marriage. A situation that happened three times. Luckily, all three times someone had a basement, or a small shed, or once, a tent on a beach, that they could use. And the tent story brought about another curve on the crooked road:

"Remember when we lived in that tent for the summer, while I went to find enough work to bring us a house again?"

"How could I forget. We ate fish from the Ocean every single day. And clams. And Oysters, and whatever else we could find. The kids thought it was great. For them it is a good memory."

He felt her hand tense underneath his. They had tried to make it an adventure for the kids, but it wasn't easy on the Adults.

"I know. Good thing you were a great cook and loved the outdoors. That farm background sure came in handy."

"That's only because you city kids think food comes already filleted, butchered, or cut up into hamburger. You would have died on the Oregon trail."

It was an old saying between them, no less true now, then it was when it was first said on a cold Pacific Beach; while laying huddled together on one side of the tent.

"Remember the toilet?"

Laughter came again.

"How could I forget? I had to lug that thing to the dumpster, fill the bags up with lime to kill the smell and bacteria. A five gallon bucket with plastic garbage bags inside, changed after every poo. Then I had to replace the seat back on top every time. You seem to have left that chore for the City Kid."

"We had chamber pots in rural Canada, and it was always the boys that had to take them out the next day. So I was just keeping tradition alive."

She squeezed his hand tighter. She knew how hard that toilet was on him. He vowed when they left that tent for their new apartment, that neither she, nor the girls would ever have to use that thing again. Flush toilets only. He kept his vow. She kept the toilet seat as a reminder. The road can get crooked.

There were times that the crooked road they took almost split. Until one or the other would forgive, apologize, or say : "I am truly sorry." For both of them knew how crooked the road was, but that they didn't want to follow it with anyone else.

The laughter came and went during the night. Soft spells of loving words filled the gaps. Stories of the crooked road that looked like a straight line to love, when looked in the rear view mirror of a long life, kept them awake until just before sunrise.

When the nurse came in to bring breakfast, there wasn't a sound. Not even of breathing. They both had found the end of that crooked road. Together.

THE END

SUNSHINE'S BENCH

By Tom Di Roma

The bench belonged to Sunshine. At least that's the way he felt about it. Why? Because it was the one she sat on every day when she took her smoking breaks. This was why he was able to see her almost every day while he was outside taking pictures of vehicles on the back lot of their dealership for the company's website. And every time he spotted her, his heart and mind would go all a flutter. That's because, to him, she was the most amazing looking woman he'd ever run across.

Somewhere just over five and a half feet tall, she had a figure that was as thin as a fashion model's. Her hair, which was straight and reddish brown in color, was trimmed almost to a point against the small of her back. And then there was her face—a face which combined the most spectacular mixture of both Hispanic and Asian heritages. There was also something about the joyfulness of her laugh that made him tingle all over every time he heard it.

Too bad their ages were so far apart. She was in her early forties while he was in his mid- sixties. If only they could have met when their ages were closer together, he definitely would have tried to get to know her better. But as it was, not only was he practically old enough to be her father, he didn't have the stamina to date the way he used to.

By the way, if you're wondering why he called her Sunshine? Well, he'd always been kind of fond of affectionate nicknames. But in this case, it was also because of her overall appearance, which seemed to light up his very existence every time he saw her.

He was thinking about Sunshine when he passed two of the women from the business office returning from a trip to the ladies' room. They were talking about an accident. What accident, he wondered? Curious, he turned around and trailed them back to their area. That's when he noticed Sunshine's cubical was empty.

"Where's Helen?" he asked the two ladies. Immediately, they got uncomfortable looks on their faces. That's when it hit him — the accident they had been talking about! "Is she all right?" he asked, as concern began to eat away like a forest fire at the insides of his stomach.

One of the two spoke up. "We don't know for sure. All we know is that Johnson got a call this morning and told us that Helen was in the hospital."

"Does he know what happened?" he asked, as the forest fire in his gut continued to blaze.

The other woman spoke this time. "Some kind of car accident." Suddenly, the fire in his stomach turned into a thick, heavy sludge of fear and sadness.

"Where's Johnson now?" he asked, as he slowly eased himself down onto Sunshine's chair. Johnson was the business office supervisor.

"We think he went to the hospital to see how she's doing."

That's where I should be, he thought to himself—but why? It wasn't like he was her boyfriend or anything, but still, the way she made him feel . . .

The heck with it, he thought and stood up. I'm going to the hospital anyway! But first, he needed to figure out what to tell his boss? In the end, he said to his boss that he had a dentist appointment he had forgotten about and then left.

When he got to the hospital, he ran into Sunshine's sister, Linda, from out of town. She was heading toward the ICU. He knew it was her from the photos he had seen taped to Sunshine's cubical. He introduced himself and told her how he knew Helen.

"So you're the one who's always staring at her," she said, not with anger, but with a warm smile.

His face immediately began to heat up. "I'm so sorry if I've been making her feel uncomfortable." He couldn't look directly into Linda's eyes. Just knowing that she knew made him feel like such a creep. "It's just that . . . she's so amazing looking."

Linda, who was a little less model-like than her sister, replied, "She is, isn't she?" This time, he did look into her eyes. They remained friendly. She went on to explain, "You don't have to feel bad about it. Actually, Helen kind of likes it that you pay her so much attention."

"She does?" he replied, feeling his face turning even redder. "I didn't know she was that aware of me watching her."

"She is," replied Linda.

Usually, when he was in the back lot of their dealership taking pictures of the new cars for the website, he tried to keep his peeking at Sunshine down to a minimum. But even though he tried to be candid about it, they say you can sometimes feel when someone is watching you. He guessed she had.

While he was thinking about Sunshine, her sister asked, "You want to go and see her?"

"I wish I could, but I'm not family. I had to lie to the front desk just to get this far."

"Why, what did you tell them?"

"I said I was her stepbrother."

"Well, in that case, we'll just tell the nurses in the ICU the same thing."

She did, which was why they let the both of them in without any objections.

One look at Sunshine and he thought, she looked terrible! Both her eyes were swollen and ringed with black and blue marks, he assumed from the driver's-side airbag.

"She's extremely lucky," said one of the nurses. Seeing Sunshine lying in the bed, looking like she did, he didn't think she was very lucky. The nurse went on to explain, "Most people in her situation would have ended up with all kinds of broken bones. Somehow, she managed not to break even one."

"Can she talk to us?" he asked the nurse.

She shook her head. "Not right now; she's heavily sedated."

"I thought you said she didn't break anything?"

"She didn't, but she does have several bruises and a slight concussion." His stomach clenched when he heard this.

Stepping forward, he tentatively picked up the fingers of one of Sunshine's hands. They felt cold and leathery, almost as if they were beginning to petrify. Tears began to fill his eyes. He wanted so much to tell her how he felt, but he knew it wouldn't do any good. Even if she could hear him, the words were stuck somewhere between his brain and his mouth.

"How long will she be under?" he asked the nurse.

"We'll continue to let her sleep for the rest of today, but by tomorrow morning, she should be wide awake."

He turned to her sister. "You're going to stay a little longer, I assume?"

She nodded. "I need to ask the nurse a few more questions, but if you have to leave . . ."

"I need to get back to work," he lied. Actually, being in the ICU was making him extremely uncomfortable, especially seeing Sunshine like she was.

"Here's my card," her sister replied, handing him her business card. "It's got my cell number on it. Call me if you need anything."

He nodded then left the ICU.

Over the next couple of days, he thought about Sunshine a lot, especially whenever he'd glance at her bench. His brain refused to acknowledge there had been an accident. He kept thinking he'd see her sitting on her bench smoking as usual. But then reality would step in and he'd cringe, especially remembering how she looked in the hospital. Finally, late on the second day, he called Linda's cell. She told him that Helen was out of the ICU and in a room.

"They're going to keep her at least one or two more days just to play it safe then release her. You should go by and say hello." Immediately, panic hit him. He couldn't do that, he told himself, but just before hanging up, he heard her say, "Helen's in room 214."

Room 214 had four beds in it. Two were unoccupied. The third had a Hispanic-looking woman in it; the fourth held Sunshine. Her eyes, which were less swollen than before, were still ringed with ugly black, blue, and green bruises. They grew huge when she saw him walk through the door.

"What are you doing here?" she asked, her tone more curious than upset.

He shrugged. "I came to see how you were doing?"

Pushing down with her hands, she tried to adjust her position in the bed. She winced and made a grunting noise. He cringed thinking about how much pain she must be in. "They may be sending me home tomorrow," she said, not looking at him directly. "But I'm not sure I'm ready for that yet."

He nodded and replied, "I don't blame you." Then remembering the items he had in his hands, he said, "I've brought you a little something," then he lifted them up so she could see. One was a twelve inch tall, furry brown teddy bear; the other was a small bouquet of flowers.

A warm smile spread across her face when she saw them. "You didn't have to," she said, as he placed them on the small dresser of drawers next to her bed.

He shrugged. "I know, but it didn't feel right to visit you without bringing something."

Just then, he heard a male voice behind him say, "Here you are, honey, I got you the Latte you wanted."

Before he could turn around and see who it was, a man came around front of him carrying two cups of coffee. He placed them on the tray that was attached to the pole next to Sunshine's bed. It was her bed's eating tray. It swung back and forth on the pole, allowing the patient to eat off it, or maybe do other stuff.

When the new arrival turned to face Sunshine, he saw her visitor and asked, "Oh, who's this?"

"Sam, this is Tim McCormick. He works for our dealer's in-house advertising agency. He takes pictures of the new cars for our website."

Sam smiled at him with a toothpaste-like smile and said, "Glad to meet you," but didn't try to shake his hand or anything.

Turmoil erupted inside his gut. Obviously, Sam was her boyfriend—at least he assumed he was. He was also very handsome; blondish hair, bluish eyes, solid build, and maybe somewhere in his later thirties or early forties. Definitely, more in her age range.

He wanted to ignore Sam, but knew he couldn't. Instead, he kept a friendly smile plastered to his face as he said to the boyfriend, "Glad to meet you, too."

Then Sam turned to Sunshine and said, "Oh, by the way, I ran into your sister in the cafeteria. She was eating breakfast. She said she'll be right up as soon as she's finished."

Sunshine nodded and that's when he decided it was time for him to leave, so he said, "Well, I have to get to work now." He smiled at Sam. "Nice meeting you," then to Sunshine, added, "Hope you get better real quick." Then just before he turned to leave, he caught a glimpse of her expression. She seemed almost confused as to why he was leaving so quickly. He didn't say anything more and just left the room.

When he got into the elevator, instead of pressing the button for the first floor, he hit the button for the basement where the hospital's cafeteria was located. Once inside, he spotted Sunshine's sister, Linda, just getting up from her table. He walked over. She seemed only slightly surprised to see him. "You're here early," she said, picking up her tray and carrying it over to one of the trash containers to empty it. He followed her.

"I wanted to see Helen before I went to work. By the way," he said as she turned around to face him. "Who's Sam?"

Linda looked at him a moment before she answered. "He's her fiancé." He felt an elevator like sensation start in his stomach then make its way up to the top of his head and then back down again. She must have caught on to what he was feeling, because she said, "Don't worry about it; I don't think it's going to last."

"Why do you say that?"

She made a face, "Because he's a little too controlling for my taste. Then she smiled. "He kind of reminds me of a used car salesman." He should have been insulted, being that he was part of the car selling business, but he knew what she meant.

"So how long have they been together?" he asked.

"A little over a year."

"And they're engaged already!"

"See what I mean about him being too controlling?" He nodded then said to her what he had said to her sister about having to get to work. After giving her one of his cards and exchanging goodbyes, he left the cafeteria.

All the way to work, he drove with the thought that he didn't want Sunshine to be engaged to Sam, or anyone else, for that matter, but there was nothing he could or should do about it. This was her life and had nothing to do with him; except, every time he looked at her empty bench over the next few weeks, he'd feel the same twinge of sadness grip his stomach and chest. Then three months later, he received an e-mail from her sister.

They've broken up, was all it said.

Oh, great, he thought. What did she expect me to do now— jump her sister's bones? He had to admit that since Sunshine had returned to work, they had become closer and more open with each other. Often, they'd sit and talk about a lot of different things—sometimes mutual TV shows they watched, other times

97

sports, but most of the time, unless he brought Sam up, she wouldn't mention him. Though lately, he did notice she seemed a little less animated than usual. He guessed whatever had been happening, was leading up to their breakup, which he made believe he didn't know about until she told him.

"I'm so sorry it didn't work out," he said, giving her a gentle but sympathetic hug.

"Thank you," she replied, holding on to him for what seemed like much longer than he thought should have been appropriate. He didn't mind at all.

Afterwards, they continued being friendly towards each other, until one day she announced, "I've met someone." Once again, he felt that elevator feeling wash over him and his throat began to tighten.

"What's his name?" he asked, swallowing hard.

"It's Allen."

"What does he do?"

"He runs an insurance company."

"Where?" She named the town. It was about sixty-miles away. "And . . ." She wouldn't look at him. "He wants me to come and work for him."

The elevator began to roll again inside his chest and stomach. "When would be your last day?"

"I gave my two-week notice today." He wanted to stomp and scream and tell her not to go, but managed to keep himself in check until he could make his way inside one of the used cars parked towards the back of the lot. That's when he let his emotions flow.

On her last day in the office, he didn't go to work. Instead, he called his boss and told him he was fighting a stomach bug then stayed inside the rest of that day, plus most of the next.

Over the following six months it became easier and easier for him to look at her bench and not get choked up. Then one day, he got this wild hair of an idea. Going over to the parts department, he bought a little jar of red touchup paint and a thin brush, and on the front edge of her bench, he painted in very tiny letters the words: Sunshine's Bench.

Then one night a few months later, he was in his apartment checking his e-mails when he found one from Linda. All it said was: Helen's back in town. While he was trying to decide whether or not to ask her if she meant long term or short, he heard an almost timid knock on his apartment door. Getting up to see who it was, he opened the door and then . . .

His heart soared! Sunshine was standing on his doorstep smiling!

The end

THE GARDENER

By Kevin Hughes

There was no way on God's green earth, even if there isn't a God, that she would ever forget the first day they met. He was tall, lanky, spindly almost, but pretty. In a masculine sort of way. She watched as he carried a fifty Gallon Drum out to the garden behind his house, and then another, and then another. By himself.

When he brought the fifth barrel back to the garden, he stopped long enough from his work to take off the lid from the barrel. He dipped his hands in and took a good long drink. Her mind did the math almost without thinking:

Fifty five gallons at a little over eight pounds a gallon= 460 pounds, rounded up just a bit.

"Shit!"

Was all she said out loud. She had just watched a man carry five four hundred plus pound barrels more than 200 yards, with about the same amount of effort she could carry a 20 pound bag of chicken feed the same distance. She knew a lot of strong men and boys, after all, they did live in the country... where hard work replaced gyms, or sports. But she didn't know anyone, not even her Uncle Henry who had won the Strong Man Contest at the Highland Games, six years in a row. Alas, a ruptured disc, and a

100

split gut put an end to that streak; who could have carried full barrels that far. Her Aunt Elsie said it was a godsend, as now Uncle Henry is only as strong as two men, not five, and not likely to lift anything much heavier than a pint.

When the new neighbor had stopped to take a drink, she had somehow found her body (with out her permission, or awareness) had migrated over to the wooden fence separating her Father's property from what used to be the Old Ferguson's place. The Ferguson's had finally taken their eldest daughter up on her annual invitation to come live at their big house in Minneapolis. Five generations had lived on that 100 acre plot, and now, a stranger.

"Hello, Neighbor."

His voice caught her off guard. It was a sweet "high tenor" that clashed with the rather striking straight cut lines of his body, which, by her reckoning, should have held a baritone with depth and dark spots in it. It thrilled her, like hearing a flute when you expected a saxophone- not bad, just different.

"Hello."

She cursed herself for not thinking of something more clever to say. Something to prolong the conversation and bring him closer to the fence between them. She need not have worried, for he wiped his brow with a bright kerchief, carefully placed the lid back on the water barrel, and loped (there is no other word, he must have covered a good ten feet with each stride, not an ounce of hurry, but a ton of efficiency in every step).

He stopped just a few feet from her, and one of those long, stringed with muscle, arms sort of floated out to shake her hand. Once again her body acted without her consent or advice, her hand floated up gently to meet his strong fingers in mid air. Their hands didn't shake at all, instead they seem to have, well, roosted in mid air. Neither letting go, except to fall - entwined, to rest on the fence rail. As comfortable as two doves snuggling against the wind.

For a moment she forgot about the tall lanky man, to stare at their two hands resting just in front of her work blouse on the wooden rail. Admiring how they seemed to compliment each other, both strong work hardened competent hands covered with the rough skin such work requires. Yet, they felt soft to the touch, welcome to the feel, and comforting to them both. So she was again caught off guard when he spoke.

"My name is Kevin. I am a gardener."

The way he said: "I am a Gardener," sounded almost angelic. Like it was more than an occupation, or profession, but a calling. For some reason a thought flitted across her mind: "He isn't a Gardener, he is thee Gardener." Later, she would come to believe that with all her heart.

His smile stayed as gently in place on his face, as his hand stayed wrapped around hers- calmly waiting for her reply. She put her other hand on top of his, to hold it firmly in place between her two palms, before she was able to look up at his smile.

"My name is Debbie. I help my Mom and Dad with the cows and chickens, and tend our garden. "

She didn't lift her hand, preferring to use her cute pointed chin, and dimpled cheeks to tilt her head in the direction of her truck garden. The lanky man's eyes followed that tilt to see almost half an acre of herbs, vegetables, and flowers growing. His smile grew a bit wider.

"That, dear Debbie, is a very nice garden. Very nice indeed."

She blushed a bit. She was proud of her garden, but not used to compliments about it. Oh, sure, her Mom and Dad both agreed that she had a "green thumb", and therefor turned the gardening chores over to her when she was only ten. She thought it was just another chore they wanted to shed trying to keep all the chickens and cows cared for. It didn't take her long to figure out that the garden was her second home. She felt comfortable there. Life started there, in the ground, from nothing. With care, love, and attention, plants, just like people, tended to grow strong, straight, and sweet. She felt that when she gardened.

"Thank you. Are you going to have a Garden back here too? The Ferguson's only grew hay, and a few rows of corn back here. "

The lanky man turned (without letting go of either of her hands) looked back over the 100 acres stretching all the way to the tree lined creek. This time his smile changed to hold a dream along with her presence.

"Oh, yes. A marvelous garden. A teaching garden. A feeding garden. A place where food is healthy, unprocessed, and fresh."

She heard the iron in his words. Whatever dream was filling his vision, it was complete in his mind. It made her want to help grow things.

"What is a teaching garden?"

"Oh, I am sorry. I got ahead of myself. When I lived in the Big City, I listened to all the young people teaching classes on how to read labels on bottles, cans, and boxes. (She smiled at the way he said: "All the young people", as if he were any older then her twenty two years). I thought to myself:

"If they only knew food comes without a label. A tomato, potato, grape, onion, carrot, peas, or beans, tell you both what it is, and what is in it. No label needed."

That is when I decided to buy this place. I am a Gardener. Not a luddite. I shall used solar energy to run my irrigation pumps. I shall use some greenhouses to grow certain plants and fruits that would other wise be out of season. And I shall use modern effective techniques for land management. But...I shall also use the natural methods that Nature had developed over years and years to help plants grow too.

Then, I shall teach as many of those young folks as I can, how healthy, tasty, and rewarding real food without labels, can be."

By this time in his impromptu speech, his eyes were alight, his grip on her hand had grown firm, as if they had just grafted their two hands to join together as one soul. She found her eyes matching the intensity of the vision he described. She wanted to be a part of it, a part of him.

"Are you going to need help?"

This time, his eyes burned with a different vision, one even more powerful, and he turned that laser like gaze on her. She returned it, unflinching, quenching the laser into a bright flame.

"Yes. Yours."

She watched him leap over the fence with about as much effort as she would have used to skip to her garden, and with the same ferocious joy she had heading to her garden. Except his joy was all focused on her.

Now side be side, the walked towards her Mom and Dad's house. Their hands having never parted, even when he leaped the wooden fence like it was a discarded shoebox laying in his way.

"What should we say to your parents?"

"I shall tell them."

"Tell them what?"

" I found my Gardener. I am moving in tonight."

Love had been planted. The garden would bloom.

THE END

THE 127AB-LOVE NEURAL TRACE

By Kevin Hughes

Bob set the cycle to follow the neural network of thought 127AB-LOVE.

Stephanie, lightly tranced by the effects of the tracer molecules, merely smiled. Out loud she said:

"That's all I had to do? Just think one thought about Kevin- and the Neurotracker does the rest?"

Bob smiled. He knew she was just trying to understand how it worked. As simple as it sounded to explain, he knew just how complicated and precise the system was. Until GOOGLE invented the first Quantum Computer something like this wasn't even possible. Without the genius of Mrs. Balzack (He always wondered why she would rather be called Mrs. Balzack intstead of Dr. Balzack. When he saw her first experiments with the emotional tunnels leading back from a single thought- he knew.)

"Stephanie, as you were told in the briefing, a faint trail of every thought you ever thought, exists in your mind. You want to know if you really love Kevin. So all you have to do is think of Kevin, any thought will do. A memory, the affect of his name on a single neuron, or a good or bad thought, like your first kiss, or a fight that lingered, will lead us back to all thoughts of Kevin.

The 127AB-LOVE node is not a single trace, it is how you "feel" about all traces of Kevin…over time. When the trail is mapped, the node will light up with your true feelings. It is false color, but we have done so many of these now the chart you were given will match how you really feel.

Rose was the color of true love. Green was the color of comfortable, but no love. Purple was jealousy. Black meant you were fooling yourself. And White, well white meant the worst emotion of all- indifference. It only takes a few minutes, so just relax."

Stephanie did just that.

Bob looked at the node as it formed. There were a lot of traces to Kevin in Stephanie's mind. But strangely enough, no traces of the echo of Kevin's responses in her auditory or sexual lobes. It was difficult for Bob to believe that someone could care that much for someone- as Stephanie's Neural Network clearly showed- and not have sensory input other than some light touches and caresses. None of the filtering nodes that Highly Religious People, or the very rare Asexual human being used to deny physical contact were lit up either.

It was the most uncomplicated picture of Love that Bob had seen in his twenty two years of working the NeuralNetwork of

127AB-LOVE. It was truly an example of unconditional love. As he already knew it would; the node glowed a vibrant Rose color.

He handed the results to Stephanie. She looked at the Rose pattern, looked up at Bob, then giggled a still slightly high sounding squeal:

"I knew it. I knew I loved Kevin!"

"I know you do. Let me tell you Stephanie, I have been doing this for decades and that chart of your 127 AB-LOVE pathway is the most remarkable one I have ever seen. You truly love Kevin, just as he is. What a lucky guy. "

Stephanie looked up a bit confused, but not by the tracer molecules, but by Bob's last comment.

"Bob...Kevin's my cat!"

The end

MIRACLE ON ROCKY RIVER ROAD

By Kevin Hughes

The All Girls Catholic School let out at the same time every day-3:20 PM. Some of the girls in their Blue skirts- matched with white blouses and covered with a Grey Vest- took the School Busses to go home. A significant number however, took the Public Bus which had a Bus Stop just out in front of the School. Every weekday morning, and every weekday afternoon, about a hundred of the Uniformed Beauties stood chattering at the Bus Stop.

Some of the more daring would roll up the top of their blue pleated skirts, to reveal their dimpled knees. A few would roll them up further, revealing some smooth velvety thigh and risking not only the admiring eyes of teens driving by, but the scorn of the pious among them. Many a rolled skirt had been reported (on the sly) to the Nuns who were guardians of the purity of their flock. And the rolling would stop, at least until warm weather, youth, or a hot guy passed by.

Some of the more rebellious among them would not only roll their skirts up, but undo a button or two on their white blouses. Some would even try to reach REBEL status by lighting up a cigarette, trying to maintain a cool composure and feigned indifference to the consequences if caught. But a pair of plain black shoes stuffed with feet covered with Navy Blue stockings was ready at all times to quash a cigarette into the grass at a moments notice.

Sweet sixteen was abundant to every passer by in the stance, hairdos, and limited makeup worn by the gaggle at the bus stop. Youth gave them a beauty that makeup would not yet enhance, but merely hide their prettiness. Some girls were tall, some short, some full figured, some still waiting for gangly to turn into statuesque. All hands and feet and bony knees, waiting for the ten or fifteen pounds that will flesh them out from cute to attractive.

Among those hundred or so Public Bus but Private School commuters was a shy confident girl. No, that is not an oxymoron. She was truly independent. She had to be. She was only awkward around guys. Not uncommon for a sixteen and half year old Junior at an All Girls Catholic School. There were only three men in the whole school: one Basketball Coach, one Counselor, and one Band/Choir Master- and all three were Priests.

The only time the girls came across any of the male of the species, was at the "Mixers" with the other two All Boy's Schools, and the other All Girl's School. Those mixers were heavily chaperoned, took place only eight times the whole school year, and no one missed any of them. The Christmas Formal, and the Prom, being the only two that cost money. Those were the only two where you had to have a date to go to. The shy confident girl had missed both those dances her first two years- and this year was shaping up to be no different.

She shrugged her head, tossing her curls in perky little hops across her head, and wondered if she would be one of those women that claimed with pride that they never went to their Prom. A false Pride, but a real claim. It made her smile, as she pictured herself saying that out loud to her True Love. Like all teen age girls, a Prince was always somewhere in the Future. Maybe even hers.

And then the miracle happened. It took a while. Almost two weeks. Not because of her, but him. For he was shy too. He walked on the other side of Rocky River Road, a road so busy, so crowded, and so dangerous to cross, that it may well have been a moat built by the Nuns to keep testosterone filled passerby's from approaching the gaggle of fresh beauties standing at the Bus Stop.

It did stop many a young boy (and a few young men too) from daring to do much more than look across the street and wave at some young girl that caught their eyes. Sometimes a few braver sort would yell across to the girls, and a kind of challenge/response game would start. To end in either embarrassment or simply drowned out by traffic, or ground to halt by the arrival of one of the busses. Sometimes both sides of the street were so caught up in their own activities or thoughts that the other side of the street might as well have been on the other side of the moon. But not today.

He was a tall gangly kid. His strength and athleticism hidden by his wiry scaffold, and lose fitting drapery. He wasn't what you would call a sharp dresser even though he had the sharp edges to his features to make those kinds of clothes hang with pride.

111

Instead he wore garish colored sweat pants, outlandish shirts, and simple grey pullover sweaters. Often the gaggle of girls would giggle at his outfits, making his blush at their pointing fingers and pointed comments clash with his sweatpants. One girl stared at him with a gentle smile on her face.

It was the shy confident girl we talked about earlier. She would look over at him the whole time he passed by the bus stop. Turning her head to track him as he walked by. He would wave, smile, wave again…but she never returned the wave, only the smile. He couldn't figure it out. She was obviously interested in him (or so he hoped). She was the cutest girl out there - in his opinion.

He loved her auburn curls that bounced like little curly cues of silk when she turned her head or the wind blew. He loved her dark sunglasses that gave a sense of style, mystery, intrigue to her presence. She was five foot three or four, and curved in that girl next door meets the beginning of beach bunny way. Her smile was a beacon that beckoned as she tracked his progress across the moat.

The girls around her noticed her tracking the gangly kid in the horrid outfits- teasing bordering on bullying started soon after. Within a week, it reached across the moat to include the gangly kid himself. He would blush furiously without a single comeback remark finding its way to his lips. He would just smile at the girl he knew was watching him with intent, wave, and scurry along a bit faster. She would smile back, but never wave.

He had enough. He knew what the girls were like at his school. He knew that the girl in the dark glasses with the Shirley Temple curls was taking a lot of unkind ribbing from the rest of the flock of uniformed harpies- he had to do something. So he did.

All one hundred girls gasped. The gangly kid was going to cross the street. The girl with the dark glasses, coiled curls, lifted her hands to her mouth to cover her fear. She heard the shrieks of the other girls as the gangly kid narrowly missed on car, then another, and yet a third, before he made it to the bus stop. The girls cheered spontaneously - and he found himself bashfully acknowledging their cheers.

Then he turned and walked directly to the girl he had seen two weeks ago for the first time, and dreamt about ever since. She tilted her head up to watch as he waked towards her. She put out both her hands in the most graceful invitation to be held that he had ever seen. His hand reached out to slide into her palms like two pieces of lego, with a solid click of joining.

"Hello."

Her voice was everything he could have imagined: soft, kind, sweet.

"Hi. My name is Mark. I...I...I er...saw you looking at me from across the street, but you never answered my wave. So I wasn't sure you were really looking at me. I mean I know you were looking at me, I could feel it. But you never waved back."

Mark had no clue why so many emotions were plastered on the faces of the strangely silent girls, who had gathered around him and the curly haired girl like some kind of Stonehenge feminine pillars

"You were looking at me, weren't you? I mean if you weren't I must look quite the fool."

Her hands squeezed his. He thought that must be a good sign. And he was right.

"You were right. I was looking at you. I didn't wave because I didn't see it."

"What?"

"Mark. I am blind."

"But...but...but...how...I mean...what?"

"I was looking at you. I saw you that first day two weeks ago. I kept hoping you would come over and say Hello. But you just kept walking."

"You're blind. How could you see me?"

"Mark, I am blind. But love is not."

Some girls fainted. Some screamed. Two of them ran to get the Nuns. Some just knelt and prayed. Some were so flummoxed that words ceased. All of them were crying. Except for the girl with the dark glasses and the gangly kid in the red sweatpants.

Still holding hands facing each other, Mark and the curly haired girl continued pouring into one another.

"What's your name?"

"Portia."

"Well, Portia, if you can see me, what do I look like?

"Love."

THE END

Manufactured by Amazon.ca
Bolton, ON

21190526R00069